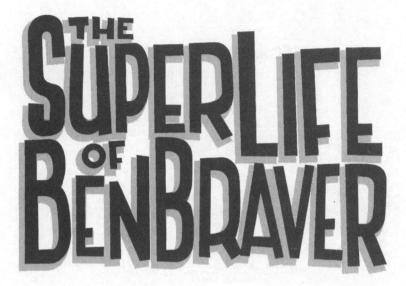

THE SUPER LIFE OF BEN BRAVER

FOR MY PARENTS...

SQUARE
FISH

An imprint of Macmillan Publishing Group, LLC
175 Fifth Avenue, New York, NY 10010
mackids.com

Square Fish and the Square Fish logo are trademarks of Macmillan and are used
by Roaring Brook Press under license from Macmillan.

Our books may be purchased in bulk for promotional, educational, or business use.
Please contact your local bookseller or the Macmillan Corporate and
Premium Sales Department at (800) 221-7945 ext. 5442 or by email at
MacmillanSpecialMarkets@macmillan.com.

Library of Congress Control Number: 2017944678

ISBN 978-1-250-29434-0 (paperback) / ISBN 978-1-250-14326-6 (ebook)

Originally published in the United States by Roaring Brook Press
First Square Fish edition, 2019
Square Fish logo designed by Filomena Tuosto

1 3 5 7 9 10 8 6 4 2

AR: 4.1 / LEXILE: 580L

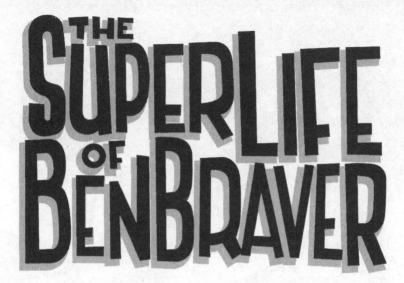

THE SUPER LIFE OF BEN BRAVER

Written and Illustrated by
Marcus Emerson

SQUARE
FISH

ROARING BROOK PRESS

New York

f I kept a diary, that would've been my entry for the day.

Super dark, right?

It's kinda hard not to be when you're standing on a burning building, staring into the gigantic eyeballs of a Godzilla-size, evil version of yourself that wants to squash you like a bug.

Not my best day ever.

All that going on, and what was the only thing on my mind?

Was I wearing clean underwear?

. . . I know, right?

Special thanks goes out to my mom for that one. She's always prepping for the worst, like, in the event of a horrible accident or maybe my untimely death.

My gravestone will say, "Here lies Ben Braver, buried in the tightest of tightys and the whitest of whiteys."

And then I remembered I was wearing black underwear.

Crisis averted . . . except for the giant me-beast facing me down. One thing at a time, though, right?

The heat of the fire crawled up my back. The building trembled as the roof fell apart behind me.

Students and teachers screamed at me from the courtyard. Well, not at *me* me, but the *giant* me crushing trees beneath his feet.

I was running out of time, and I knew it. I had ten, *maybe* twenty, seconds before the hundred-foot-tall monster started throwing his truck-size fists at me.

Like, there was a good chance I wasn't gonna see the next sunrise, so *of course* the creamy, brain-filled center of my skull chose *that exact moment* to flash my life before my eyes.

Flash wasn't the right word. *Unfolded like a book with drawings* was probably a better way to put it.

It all started on that hot summer night eight months ago. . . .

CHAPTER ONE

My whole life changed all because I wanted a peanut butter cup.

It was the end of summer vacation, and I was in my basement binging the second season of that cheesy Batman show from the sixties starring the greatest of greats, Adam West.

I was the little piggy that stayed home that summer, soaking up old TV shows like a sponge. They were a nice distraction from how boring my life was after my best friend, Finn, moved away only three months before.

His dad got a job across the country that needed his family to relocate, like, stupid fast.

One weekend Finn and I were building cabins in the woods; the next weekend he was gone.

I tried to make it a "no bummer summer," but even with the awesome title, it was still a vacation slathered in lamesauce without my best friend.

Before starting the third season of *Batman*, I decided I needed a snack encounter of the peanut butter kind.

That, and I probably needed to air myself out. Clothes get funky pretty fast when you're in a dark basement all day.

I hopped on my bike, rode to the gas station a block over, and slapped four quarters on the counter like I was a big shot with cash.

"A package of your finest peanut butter cups, good sir!" I said.

The gas station clerk groaned.

The little bell jingled behind me as the flimsy screen door slammed shut. I slipped my snack into my back pocket, grabbed my bike, and pedaled for home.

A decent end to a decent day.

And then some kid shouted for help in the distance.

It sounded like *"Halp!"*

I shrugged it off and kept riding. I had only about five minutes until my peanut butter cups melted in my back pocket.

BTW, peanut butter cups are my fave. I *love* them, but . . . would I marry one? Probably not, but only because my second love, the PB&J sammie, would get jelly. Get it? Jelly?

I wonder what a peanut butter cup wedding would even look like. . . .

Um . . . nevermind.

Although my dad calls me creative, and my mom says I'm a free spirit, I, Ben Braver, am really just the most normal eleven-year-old boy in the world.

Nothin' special here.

I've got hobbies like everyone else. I love riding my bike through the woods. I play video games like it's my job. I'm a movie buff, too. My favorites are awful sci-fi ones from the fifties with titles like *The Day of the Triffids*, and where they say things like *"Her brain kept alive by experimental science!"*

And I read books . . . *comic* books.

Honestly, comics are *more* than a hobby. They're my way of life. It's supes nerdy, but I secretly dream of becoming a superhero.

I bet you do, too.

Ever stare out the car window and imagine yourself flying through the clouds? Running at superspeed? Saving the day?

Remarkable. That's what I'd be if I were a superhero.

If I were, then maybe kids would actually notice me.

But I'm not. So they don't.

I'm the soggy fries on the bottom of the carton, the powder at the end of a box of cereal, the last kid standing when teams are picked.

Unremarkable.

That's me.

But it's all about the journey, right? That's the part of comics that sucks me in. Being a superhero is more than having powers—it's about the struggles and the choices heroes have to make. It's about deciding to do the right thing even when the right thing is the hardest thing to do.

And as I slowed my bike on the bridge near my house, I knew I suddenly had my own choice to make: go home and dig into my peanut butter cups or save that kid shouting for help.

CHAPTER TWO

I plopped down on the couch, ready for another six hours of TV. The remote was in my hand, but my thumb couldn't press Play, like it was cosmically blocked from doing it.

Because I knew I had just made the *wrong* choice.

Adam West looked at me with disappointment from the paused television screen.

All I wanted to do was watch TV, but something told me I *needed* to get back out there.

"Flippin' eggs." I sighed, tossing my snack aside. And then I headed back to the garage to get my bike.

I think it's what Adam West would've done.

Soon I was coasting down the sidewalk toward the cries for help.

I rounded the bend and saw a group of kids circled around two boys—a bully named Dexter Dunn and his victim, Caden Cameron.

Dexter was kind of the neighborhood bully. "Kind of" because the hermit barely ever came out of his house, but when he did . . . he was a Grade A jerk.

His family was mysterious, mostly staying indoors. They were a work-from-home, school-at-home kind of family.

Dexter had an older sister, too, but I think she was sent away to military school or something a few years ago. Either that or his family hid her in the attic for some reason.

The boy in trouble was Caden Cameron. He sometimes took his dog to play in the creek under the bridge.

"Stop it! You're gonna hurt him!" Caden shouted.

"He's fine! He likes it!" Dexter said as he yanked the poor animal's leash around like it was a toy.

My three-point plan of attack was this:

RIDE IN ALL SMOOTH AND CHARMING.

WAD!

CALL DEXTER OUT FOR BEING A WAD.

SHOWER IN THE PRAISE OF MY NEW FANS.

Boom.

Day saved. *Next day, please.*

I needed to get everyone's attention by making an entrance.

Hero work demanded theatrical entrances.

I rode and then kicked back on the pedal to slide my tire around in a half circle, skidding to a stop right in front of my future fans in a cloud of dust and awesome.

If that was how it went down, then it would've *rocked* . . . but that *was not* how it went down, so it *did not* rock.

Instead, my back tire swooped around and hit a crack in the pavement. My bike stopped, but my body didn't. I flipped off the front like a wet noodle.

Kids scrambled out of the way as I tumbled toward Dexter and Caden. I landed flat on my back, looking up as everyone stared down at me.

"I'm good," I said, getting to my feet. And then I pointed at Dexter. "What's *not* good is you messing with Caden's dog. Give him back."

"It's a her," Caden whispered.

"C'mon, man, work with me here," I said.

"But my dog's a girl," Caden whined. "And you called her a he."

"Fine, give *her* back."

"Make me," Dexter said menacingly.

"What?"

"*Make! Me!*"

Whoa, wait . . . Dexter was just supposed to give the dog back. Challenging me was *not* part of my three-point plan of attack! Didn't he know that?! I probably shoulda told him.

"Just give the dog back. You really wanna do this?" I said. "You can't make friends, so you gotta steal animals?"

"*I can make friends*," Dexter said through his teeth.

A chilly breeze swept past my shins.

I began to babble. My mouth ran whenever I got nervous.

"Are you even a dog person?" I asked, swallowing

hard. "I see you more as a *fish* kind of guy. Or whatever kind of pet that doesn't require a lot of brain cells to take care of. Y'know, things at the bottom of the food chain. Start with a plant and work your way up. Or a rock! Did you know there are pet rocks?"

The kids around us giggled, which only made Dexter angrier. He dropped the dog's leash.

Saved the dog.

Nailed it.

And then Dexter fixed his eyes on me. His creepy, *cloudy* eyes.

Super not normal.

He shoved me. "So you're the funny kid, huh?"

I planted my foot and caught myself. "No! I'm not the *funny* kid! I'm the *Braver* kid! Get it? Whatever. Caden got his dog back, and that's all I cared about. So while this has been fun, I'm out."

I reached for my bike, but Dexter shoved me again, obviously wanting to top his night off with a gentlemanly scuffle.

"Dude, seriously," I said. "Knock it off."

"I'll knock *you* off, Ben *Dover*," Dexter said.

"*Nice*," I said. "If I ever need a snarky comeback, I'll come and find you so I know what *not* to say."

Dexter tried pushing me again, but I slapped his hands out of the way before he could.

His skin was like ice! It was so cold that my fingers burned even though I touched him for only a second.

Gasps came from the kids around us.

Caden and his dog were already gone.

So much for showering in the praise of my new fans.

The area around Dexter became engulfed in shadow, but a shadow that floated in the air like smoke. The concrete cracked under my feet.

The whites of Dexter's eyes were gone. They were just black sockets on his face.

Super *terrifyingly* not normal.

The last thing I remember that night was a burst of white light before the sharpest cold I'd ever felt in my life.

And I never even got to eat my peanut butter cups.

CHAPTER THREE

My head snapped to attention like I was struggling to stay awake in class.

Except I wasn't in class.

I was standing at the front of a huge church, dressed in a black tux.

My family filled the pews on the left side of the room, wearing their best smiles. Aunts, uncles, cousins . . . *all* of them.

Oh, man . . . was I watching my own funeral?

"Ben, are you okay?" a girl's voice said to my right. "You look like you're about to pass out."

"Uh, yeah, I'm fine," I said, shaking my head out of the fog. "I had this weird dream where I saved a kid's dog, and then it got cold. . . ."

"Stop daydreaming at our wedding!"

"... our what?"

I looked at my bride. She was a five-foot-tall peanut butter cup wearing a white wedding dress and bright red lipstick.

I glanced around. The other side of the church was filled with other smiling peanut butter cups.

"Huh ... so *this* is what it would look like," I whispered.

"Anyone object to these two gettin' hitched?" the pastor behind us asked, arms outstretched.

The church doors burst open. A skinny peanut butter and jelly sandwich wearing heels came running down the aisle.

"I do!" the PB&J sammie screamed. "Ben is in love with me! Not that chocolate-covered floozy standing next to him!"

My bride pressed her lips together, hoisted her dress up, and scurried down the steps. *"Chocolate-covered floozy?* At least I'm gluten-free, which is more than I can say about you, ya jelly-filled tart!"

"*Ohhhhh!*" the spectators shouted.

"*How dare you!*" the PB&J sammie shrieked as she slapped the peanut butter cup across the face.

That's when my bride *freaked.* Clenching her fists and letting out a battle cry that would scare a baby, she let loose a flurry of fists, pummeling the soft white bread of the sammie.

People—and candy—from both sides of the aisle jumped up and down, holding money over their heads, placing bets on who was going to win the fight.

It was . . . *odd.*

The PB&J sammie took off one of her heels and whacked the peanut butter cup on the head. My bride retaliated by thrusting her hand into the sammie's chest and ripping out her still-beating peanut heart.

I dropped to my knees and tried to scream. . . .

With a tiny yelp, I shot up in my bed back at home.

I was in my bedroom.

At least, I *thought* I was in my room.

Huge machines surrounded my bed. Retro computer monitors flickered and came to life as they beeped at me.

I tried rubbing my eyes, but my fingers had wires taped to them that snaked through my sheets to the medical equipment.

Was I still dreaming? Was my brain being kept alive by experimental science?

The medical gear beeped louder and faster as I panicked. My blanket felt like it weighed a hundred pounds as the room closed in around me.

"Mom!" I shouted, but my throat was dry, so it came out only as a whisper. *"Dad!"*

Footsteps pounded down the hall. Relief poured over me as my mom stepped through the door.

"He's awake!"

CHAPTER FOUR

9 p.m.

Sunday.

The living room.

My parents sat on each side of me while a ninety-year-old man with a huge scar across his face told me the craziest junk I'd ever heard in my life.

After Dexter went all "horror movie" on me, I was taken to the hospital. I was there for only a few hours before the old man with the scar brought in "his people" to take me home to recover.

My parents agreed to it because of how strange the situation was. Dad said that half of my body was frozen in a block of ice when they found me.

The team that transported me from the hospital stayed in a giant bus outside my parents' house.

Whatever Dexter did put me in a coma for *three days.*

The old man was Donald Kepler. He was the headmaster of a boarding school called Kepler Acad-

DONALD
KEPLER

emy, which was—get this—"*a secret school for kids with special abilities.*"

He was tall and lanky and decked out in black. Black suit, black shirt, black tie, and black coat. Ninety-nine percent sure that dude slept in a coffin.

His bushy eyebrows and noggin hair were, ironically, white.

Kepler took a breath and exhaled slowly. "I'm speaking about individuals who have developed special abilities. . . . I hesitate to call them this, but you would say they were . . . *superpowers*." He said the word like it revolted him.

I stared at the old man on the couch. "Stop it," I said, not in a mean way, but in a *"whatever"* kind of way. "You're messing with me, right?"

Kepler shook his head.

I laughed. "You almost got me! Nice prank, dude. Way to get Dexter in on it, too."

"I didn't believe Mr. Kepler at first, either," Dad said, "but he's been here for three days showing us enough evidence that . . . yes, I believe he's telling the truth."

"There's no other way to explain what happened to you," Mom said.

"What, with Dexter?" I said, racking my brain to come up with an explanation about how I got trapped in ice, but I had nothing.

"Dexter's *abilities* manifested," Kepler said, folding his hands on his lap. "It happens to all with abilities around the age of middle school."

I was actually speechless.

". . . which is why my academy starts at sixth grade. My school helps children with their new abilities."

I couldn't believe what I was hearing. "Okay, Professor X, that's already been done. Is your school in a mansion, too?"

"Why would my school be in a mansion?"

I guess Kepler didn't know about the X-Men.

"Okaaay, so you're telling me you started a school for people with superpowers?"

"Abilities."

"Right, *abilities*," I said, making air quotes. "So where are all these superpowered kids in the world? There's no such thing as superheroes."

"Obviously, it's all very secret. It *must* be. It's far too dangerous for the world to know we exist. My school teaches students to harness their talents and learn to control them. An uncontrolled ability is a danger to the individual. It can be quite deadly. You know that first-hand."

"Why are you even here?" I asked.

Kepler answered immediately. "To offer you a spot at my school."

"*Come on!* This is a joke, right?" I turned my face to the ground. "*Or* I'm still dreaming. . . . Mom, if I told you I married a peanut butter cup, would you be cool with it?"

Mom made a face. "*What?*"

I set my mug on the coffee table and then tossed the old man a thumbs-up. "Thanks for saving my life and stuff, but I think I'm still feeling kinda sick, y'know, from the *coma*."

"Ben, where are you going?" Dad said as I walked away.

"Back to bed," I said. "This whole thing is because you all know how much I love comics and superheroes. It's not funny anymore."

I made sure to slam the door loud enough for the whole neighborhood to hear.

The roof outside my bedroom window.

My "go to" place when I want to be alone.

Stars shimmered like glitter in the clear sky. I knew I couldn't see every star in the galaxy, but it almost felt like I could.

Kepler's bus sat in the street in front of my house, the shadows of his employees walking around inside it.

I was still reeling at the prank my parents pulled. They knew I was ob-sessed with comics. How could they make fun of me like that?

A prank on that level had to take some crazy planning. Getting all those kids in on it. Dex-ter. Hiring an actor with a fake scar. Renting a bus. They even changed the dates on all the cell phones in the house to trick me into thinking I was actually out for three days.

"Nice night," a voice suddenly said right next to me. It was the old man.

I flinched. The man was sneaky like an old ninja. "Don't you need to get that bus back to the . . . bus . . . rental . . . store."

Nailed it.

"Why must you be such a hardheaded child?" Kepler asked, obviously impatient and annoyed, like your typical old guy with a grudge against all kids.

"Because I hate feeling like a butt, and that's all your little prank is doing," I said. "I'm forever telling my friends about how I wish aliens would abduct me to be the last starfighter! Or how awesome it'd be to have a time machine DeLorean! Or how it'd be super rad if people had *real* superpowers." I paused. "I'm just tired of getting teased about all that. . . ."

Kepler sucked air through his nose. "You're right. This hasn't been fair to you."

Finally.

He was gonna fess up and admit it was all a bad joke.

INCOMING
HISSY FIT...

24

Kepler continued. "I've been at this for so long that I sometimes forget how unrealistic it might sound to the uninitiated."

That was it. I couldn't take any more. I stomped my feet on the roof and shouted like a kid throwing a tantrum. "*Go! Away!*"

The shingles under my feet slipped out, and before I knew it, I was sliding down the roof.

Falling off my house—what a perfect way to end my night.

But then, in an instant, my body stopped. Kepler was on the edge of the roof, but *behind* me, keeping me from falling.

"I have you," he said.

"But . . ." I said, trying to find my voice. "How'd you get behind me so fast?"

The old man smiled. "I think you know how."

My mind was blown. Did that ninety-year-old man really just save my life by using a superpower? Could he have been telling the truth, and this *wasn't* some lame prank?

I suddenly had questions—*lots of them*—but all I could say was, "No way."

I got my balance back, and we both sat on the edge of the roof, our feet dangling over the side.

My mouth finally caught up with my thoughts. "Is it superspeed? Is that your power?"

"The stars look lovely from up here," Kepler said

softly, ignoring my question. "Have you given any thought to my invitation?"

"Um, not really, but that was before the whole 'falling off the roof' thing."

"My academy is not open to the public, nor does it even *exist* to the public. And I can assure you, this is no prank."

"But why me? *Are you telling me I have a super-power?!*" I asked, feeling blood rush to my face.

It's the thing *every kid* always dreamed about! A thing that's *impossible*, but there I was, sitting next to an old guy telling me that, yeah, maybe it *was* possible.

If superpowered people really existed, then *of course* they would be kept secret.

"What's my power?" My voice squeaked like a mouse.

Kepler laughed. "I don't know. Talents are random and can't be predicted."

By *not* saying I had them, he was pretty much saying that I *did*.

Aw, yeah!

"Ben, I'd like very much for you to attend my school. I don't use this word often, but I *do* believe it's your *destiny* to come to the Lodge. You're full of spirit, and that's something I think the academy is in desperate need of. Everyone will be excited to meet you."

"But they'll all have powers already. I won't."

"Not true. Most sixth graders at the academy haven't developed talents yet. You won't stand out in the least."

"But what about my parents? I'm not sure they'd let me go."

"I've spent three days convincing them. I believe they've come around. They've agreed to let you attend . . . as long as it's what *you* want."

I wasn't sure what to say. "How long is the school for?"

"Three years for middle school. You'll live at the Lodge during the school year and spend your summers here at home."

"What about vacations? Thanksgiving? Christmas? Spring break?"

Kepler paused. "Students aren't allowed to return home during the year. That much traveling is simply too risky."

I was crushed. "I won't even get to see my parents at Christmas?"

The old man shook his head.

A whole year without my parents. Ouch. "I don't know. School starts next week, and it'll be weird if I just disappeared."

I don't know why I said that. It *wouldn't* be weird to anyone because they wouldn't even notice I was gone. And without Finn, sixth grade at my normal school was gonna feel empty.

"How about this," Kepler said. "Attend for one semester. If, by Christmas, you're unhappy, then I'll send you home, no questions asked. Of course, if you don't develop a talent by then, you'll be sent home anyway."

"Some students don't develop powers?"

"Our policy is to send home the students who don't. However, it's not one we've ever used."

Kepler stood, towering over me. "It seems you have a choice to make. Stay home, and I can have your memories wiped clean of all this or . . . you can take a shot at becoming truly *remarkable*."

"You can wipe memories?"

"We have people for that. How do you think we brought you home from the hospital so easily? Nobody working that night even remembers you were there."

Typical.

Kepler pulled a pocket watch from his suit jacket. "If you give it until Christmas, you'll have lost only one semester of time."

Half a year didn't sound so bad.

Then he tossed his watch off the roof, out over the front yard.

"And you won't wipe my brain?" I asked, but no answer came.

Kepler wasn't by my side anymore. He was on the sidewalk in front of my house. With his hand held out, he caught the watch he had thrown from the roof just seconds ago.

I watched as he boarded the bus.

One word was all it took to convince me. . . .

Remarkable.

THE
REMARKABLE BEN BRAVER
SAVES THE WORLD!

OOOO... YES, PLEASE.

CHAPTER SIX

6 p.m.

Two nights later.

My parents and I were in the kitchen eating mac-and-cheese pizza and talking about Kepler Academy for the hundredth time since the old man left.

The plan was for me to leave early the next morning. The academy was sending a car to pick me up, but part of me still wasn't sure about going.

"It *is* a real school, right?" I asked, drowning my slice of pizza in a puddle of ketchup. Don't judge me.

"That's what Mr. Kepler said." Mom took the ketchup bottle and put it just out of arm's reach. "It's like a normal school but with a few specialized classes."

"It's basically a private school in the Colorado mountains," Dad said, and then he winked at me. "You'll probably grow a beard out there."

Me with a beard? Epic.

"It *sounds* like it could be a lot of fun," Mom said encouragingly. "And I know this summer hasn't been the best."

She was talking about Finn.

"Honestly," Mom said, "your father and I are a little hesitant, but Mr. Kepler and one of his employees assured us that the school is perfectly safe."

"You'll be gone all year," Dad said, "but we'll still be able to talk."

Mom went on. "Ever since you were a little kid, you've tied capes around your neck and pretended to save all your little dolls—"

"Action figures," I corrected.

"*Action figures*," Mom repeated. "You've dreamed about this. . . . And now, here it is."

I'VE SEEN SOME THINGS, MAN. YOU DON'T EVEN WANNA KNOW.

OLD BEARDED BEN

I chewed slowly, staring at my plate. A week ago, I was just a normal kid who wanted a peanut butter cup. And now I was talking about moving away from everything I knew.

My family. My home. My friends.

Oh wait, what friends?

The whole thing suddenly became real.

"Ben, are *you* okay with this?" Dad asked, setting his fork down. He could tell something was wrong.

"I don't know. . . ."

My dad leaned closer. "Your mom and I will support whatever decision you make, but we want you to know the decision is *yours*."

I said nothing.

"Because this situation *isn't* normal," Dad continued. "Until a week ago, we *knew* superpowers weren't real, but now they *are*. I wouldn't even call this a once-in-a-lifetime opportunity. It's truly *that* unique. This isn't like deciding to join the swim team."

"Do you guys think I should go?" I asked.

Mom took a deep breath. "We want you to be happy, and for you to get the most out of life. It'd be a shame to not at least *see* what the school is like . . ."

"Ben, he showed us his power," Dad said. "The people on the bus—they showed us their powers. This isn't just some fancy rich-kid school, and Mr. Kepler seems to believe you have a place there. And, if he's right . . . then it might be risky *not* to go. The worst that'll happen is you come home exactly the same."

"We want you here with us always," Mom said, "but this . . . it's too big to pass up. Too . . . *cool*. This is a school for *superheroes*! And you've been hand-selected to attend!" Her eyes got big. "You're like the Chosen One."

I got goose bumps.

"But listen," Dad said. "I'm *so* proud of you, but I'm still worried. What you did last week—standing up to Dexter—was a *good* thing . . . heroic even, but it was also *dangerous* . . . and *stupid*. You could've gotten seriously hurt."

I nodded.

Dad continued. "When you're at Kepler Academy, you'll be on your own, so you have to promise me you'll be *careful*. Be *smart*. And most important . . . be *safe*. Don't do anything stupid. Stupid could get you *hurt* . . . or *worse*. Deal?"

I held my hand out sideways. "Deal."

Dad slapped the back of my hand, and we did the secret Braver handshake we made up at the beginning of summer after Finn moved.

We spent the rest of the night tearing into pizza and trying to teach my mom the handshake. She couldn't get the hang of it, but it was cool that she tried.

I was really gonna miss them.

CHAPTER SEVEN

4 a.m.

The next morning.

My ride to the academy was waiting. When Kepler said it would be there *early*, he really meant it.

I expected some kind of top secret army vehicle to pick me up, but what I got instead was the total opposite.

A tiny, vintage Volkswagen Beetle with tinted windows sat patiently in my driveway. The lights were on, the engine was running, but there was no driver.

I stared at the inside of the car.

Dad knew I was stalling.

"Ben, it'll be okay," Dad said.

"I know," I said, acting cool.

He put his hand on my shoulder and pointed at the morning sky, still full of stars. "You know what star that is?"

"The North Star," I said.

"If you ever feel alone, just find that star. I promise you I'll look at it every single night you're gone, all right? All you have to do is glance at it. Don't even tell anyone. It's just you and your mom and me. Okay?"

I gave both of my parents a hug. They kept their

good-byes short so they wouldn't be sad. Or maybe it was the other way around.

I threw my bags in the trunk and sat in the passenger seat. The car put itself into drive, and I was off to Kepler Academy, or *the Lodge*, as Mr. Kepler called it. Still not sure why he called it that.

The GPS monitor on the dashboard said the trip was fourteen hours long, and the three PB&J sandwiches on the seat next to me told me we weren't making any unnecessary stops.

I leaned my head against the window. My mind raced as I watched blurry streetlights pass by.

What was the academy gonna be like? What other powers would students have? What was *my* power going to be? Would I really grow a beard?

It was unreal. It was like I was in a movie with all the parts of the formula.

Most stories follow a formula—three main parts called "acts 1, 2, and 3." And then a bunch of other things sprinkled on top to give it extra flavor, kind of like pizza.

Most pizza is the same—crust, sauce, meats, veggies, and then cheese on top. Some pizzas have different toppings, some have different shapes, but in the end, it's all pizza.

I took my sketchbook out of my backpack. It was brand-new, still with thick and crisp yellow pages. The only thing on it was the title I had drawn with a Sharpie: *Sketchbook of Secret Stuff.*

I doodled for what felt like hours, sketching costume and name ideas, smearing pencil lead with the butt of my palm, and blowing eraser dandruff off the paper.

I stretched out my legs, wondering how long the car had been driving. The sky was still dark, but the sun didn't rise until about six thirty anyway.

It had to have been an hour. Maybe two?

Fifteen minutes.

The clock on the dashboard said it had been only fifteen minutes.

It was going to be a long day. . . .

CHAPTER EIGHT

A female voice with a British accent woke me up.

I wiped the sleep from my eyes and mashed my face against the cold window.

YOUR DESTINATION IS AHEAD ON THE LEFT...

The sun was setting behind tall mountains as my car drove along a narrow road carved into the side of a cliff. In the valley below was a bustling city full of lights and skyscrapers. The GPS called the city Lost Nation.

Out the front windshield was a line of other tiny VW Beetles driving in the same direction. The view out the back window was the same. All students going to Kepler Academy. The girl in the car behind me waved with a smile. I waved back.

Farther down the road, tiny cars were parked in perfect lines.

That had to be it. The end of the trip.

And then I saw it.

I waited in my seat for twenty minutes as other cars dropped off their student passengers. Every time my ride lurched forward, my heart skipped a beat.

The building was huge, at least ten stories tall. Kepler called it the Lodge because I'm pretty sure that's what it used to be: a ski lodge.

When it was my turn to leave my car, I reached for the door handle, but it opened before I touched it.

"Welcome to Kepler Academy, Benjamin Braver, car three ten," a robotic voice said. *"Allow me to help with your belongings."*

A robotic octopus about the size of a milk crate waited outside my door. The robot's tentacles looked like shiny metal snakes.

"Robots, too?" I said, hoisting my backpack over one shoulder. "Crazy."

The octo-bot shut the door and popped the trunk.

"Follow me to your room," it said after grabbing my luggage and gliding past me.

Dozens of students were making their way to the front entrance with their own octo-bots. Some looked my age. Others were obviously older.

Front and center of the Lodge stood a statue of a boy battling a massive snake that coiled around him. The boy's face looked so real it was spooky.

To my left, a goat wandered the school grounds without a leash. This high in the mountains probably meant I'd see a few more wild animals than I was used to.

And the landscape was gorgeous. I'd never seen so many colors in the flower beds that lined the building. They looked out of this world.

At the top of the steps, my robot attendant pulled open one of the front doors. *"After you, Benjamin Braver."*

After rolling my shoulders and cracking my neck, I stepped through the entrance and found myself standing in a massive front lobby with an open ceiling that went up ten stories, all the way to the roof.

Dark red carpet with geometric patterns stretched across the room, under a dozen couches, and ended at a grand staircase that led to the second floor.

On the left side of the staircase was a service desk, where students were talking to some of the adult staff. On the right of the staircase was a small café called Cool Beanz, with leather chairs and wooden tables.

The lobby was so packed and filled with activity that it looked like the mall around Christmastime.

Kids followed their own octo-bots while others talked on the couches in front of the staircase.

My octo-bot turned and spoke. *"This way to room three ten, Benjamin Braver. We must hurry. The welcome ceremony begins in thirty minutes."*

"On it," I said.

I was overwhelmed. I even pinched my arm just to make sure I wasn't dreaming.

It hurt, but there I was, still standing in the middle of a school for kids with superpowers. I took a second to soak it all in.

I made it.

I was there.

And my act 2 was just beginning.

CHAPTER NINE

Instead of going to the front desk, my octo-bot led me to an elevator at the side of the massive lobby.

The dirty brass doors slid open just as I got there. The only other person waiting for the elevator stepped into it along with her own robot servant.

"Hi," I said.

"Hey," she said with a tight smile.

The elevator doors shut. Both octo-bots slid a tentacle up the wall and tapped the button for our floors. I was on three. She was on four.

The sounds from the lobby faded away, leaving us with smooth jazz, which filtered through crusty metal speakers.

The girl stared at the doors without saying a word. Sunglasses rested on the tip of her nose. And she had a beanie on her head that was pulled back enough to show her blond

hair underneath. A ukulele hung over her shoulder on her back.

I wondered what power she had.

Something to do with water? Electricity? Super-strength? Was there any way to tell?

"Dude . . . stop staring at me," she said, annoyed and watching my reflection in the metal elevator doors.

"I, uh . . . sorry," I said, embarrassed.

My face started to get all hot and sweaty as the elevator took its sweet time getting to my floor. "It's my first time here."

"It's *everybody's* first time here. At least if you're in sixth grade."

"So you're in sixth grade, too?"

She nodded but kept her eyes on the doors.

"What's your power?" I blurted out.

"Nunya."

"Oh, I, uh . . . no, I mean, what?"

The elevator doors *finally* scraped open.

"This is my floor!" I said, running out without looking back.

My octo-bot took the lead. The hallway was long and boring, with, like, an infinity of doors. It was like every hotel I've ever stayed at, complete with the bleach-and-chlorine smell that lingered in the air.

Most of the students on my floor were in their rooms, moving stuff from their luggage to their closet. Some rooms had one kid. Others had two.

My octo-bot stopped outside room 310 and opened the door.

"*The welcoming ceremony will begin shortly,*" the robot said. "*Attendance is mandatory. Report to the courtyard in twenty minutes.*"

I poked my head in. Nothing special to report. Standard hotel room. Bathroom. Shower. Couple of beds. Couple of desks. Couch. TV. The usual.

"Hello?" I called out, dragging my suitcases into the room, which smelled of stale bonfire and beef jerky.

A kid stepped around the corner. "Hi!" he said with a mouth full of food. He held out a stick of dried meat. "Want some? It's Korean BBQ–flavored."

After a day of only PB&J sammies, I was dying for something else, and the smell of his snack made me hungry. "Thanks," I said, tearing off a chunk of meat. "My name's Ben. Ben Braver."

"I'm Noah Nichols."

We stared at each other for a second.

Meeting new people is always awkward.

"So what's your power?" I asked.

Noah smiled. "Fire."

"No way. Like, you can control fire?"

Noah bobbed his head back and forth. "I mean, I

can't *control* it yet. At least not that well. What's *yours*?"

I shrugged. "I don't know."

"That's okay!" Noah said reassuringly. "Half the sixth graders here don't know what their power is yet. But that's why we're all here, right?"

It made me feel a little better knowing I wasn't the only clueless one. "How'd you find out what yours was?"

"It was on accident," Noah said. "It's *always* on accident, though."

"Did you blow something up?"

Noah laughed. "No! I, um . . ." He trailed off for a second as he headed for the door. After closing it, he spoke quietly. "It's better if I just show you. . . ."

Noah took a bite of his beef jerky and talked while he chewed. "My secret is that I can only do it after I eat jerky."

"Why?"

"I don't know." Noah grunted. He put his finger up and stared into space for a second.

Then he swooped his head down and opened his mouth, letting out a burp along with a basketball-size fireball that formed in front of his mouth.

The fireball shot up and blew a hole in the ceiling above the couch. Little crackling bits of tile fell to the floor.

"You're like a dragon!" I shouted.

Noah laughed, nodding fast. "Wanna see it again?"

"*Seriously?*" a girl shouted from above us. She pressed her face against the hole in our ceiling. "*Ew! Why does this smell like burnt salami?*"

It was the girl from the elevator. She recognized me right away.

"*You!*" she growled.

Noah and I looked at each other. We both had the same idea. We bolted for the door and ran down the hallway as fast as we could.

CHAPTER TEN

O utside in the courtyard, Noah and I stood in line for the food table, shuffling forward like zombies at an all-you-can-eat brains bonanza.

The welcoming ceremony was about to begin.

Most of the students at Kepler Academy looked totally normal. Nothing about them said "superpowers."

But others weren't so lucky.

One boy's neck was, like, three feet long. Another boy looked like he was turning into a wolf. And then there was a girl who had four extra arms . . . She could've been a one-person volleyball team.

How did the school know which kids in the world had powers and which didn't? I wondered.

I was at a place where *every* kid had a power *even* if they didn't know what it was yet. The academy had to have *some* way of figuring that out.

When Noah and I reached the food table, we each took a plate and perused the selection.

"It's *all* got bacon in it!" the large chef behind the table roared as he set down a tray of bacon-wrapped dates.

"Glen." An older woman smiled as she walked behind the table. "These dates are going to be the death of me."

"Abigail knows how to get seconds," he said to me, scooping a pile of dates onto her plate. "She deserves it, though. She makes the school grounds so pretty with all the flowers and whatnot."

The woman winked and then tiptoed away like she was breaking the rules.

Noah and I filled our plates and found an empty bench.

"Can bacon make you breathe fire, too?" I asked. "It's kind of like beef jerky."

"I don't think so," Noah said. "Never tried, though."

I barely got a bite of food before the girl from the elevator marched up to us.

"*You!*" she said accusingly. Her ukulele was still slung over her shoulder.

"Uh-oh . . ." I whispered.

"Thank you soooooo much for burning a *hole* in my floor," she said. "Hashtag, LayingTheSarcasmNiceAnd ThickSoItDoesntGoOverYourHead!"

"That's a long hashtag," Noah said.

"*He's* the one who did it!" I said, pointing at my roommate.

Noah shrunk. "Sorry."

"My whole room stinks now!" the girl said.

"I'm sorry!" Noah said again. "We can switch rooms if you want!"

"How's *that* gonna work?" she asked. "I'm on the girls' floor, and you're on the boys' floor."

"Right . . . that might raise eyebrows. People would talk," Noah said, scratching his chin. He held his plate out to the girl. "If I give you my food, will you go away?"

"Uh, first—that food's free," the girl said snidely. "And second—everything's got *bacon* in it. I'm a *vegetarian*."

Noah coughed and, just like back in our room, burped loudly. A tiny fireball crackled out and disappeared.

All the kids turned their heads to look.

Noah blinked his singed eyelashes. "Apparently, bacon *does* work like jerky."

The girl tried to keep from laughing but couldn't. Good thing, too, because I didn't think she was gonna be happy until she was standing over our beaten-up bodies.

"There's that burnt-salami smell again," she said, wrinkling her nose.

"I'm Ben," I said, reaching my hand out to shake hers.

She gave me five. "Penny Plum."

"And I'm Noah," Noah said, fist-bumping Penny. "What's your power?"

She sighed, glancing over her shoulder to make sure nobody was nearby, and then she swung the ukulele in front of her.

"I can talk to animals," she whispered, grazing her

fingers over the ukulele strings. "But only when I play the uke . . . and only small animals, y'know, mice and gerbils and stuff . . . like that one sitting next to you."

Noah and I looked at the spot between us. There, sitting perfectly still, was a small mouse.

SQUEAK.*

*TRANSLATION: "S'UP, MY DUDES? LOVELY NIGHT, ISN'T IT?"

I fell off my seat. My food flew into the grass.

Penny laughed. "He won't hurt you! Not unless I *tell* him to. . . ." She strummed her uke again but didn't say a word.

The mouse slowly turned his head and looked at me. And then it smiled.

Freaky.

"Okay, stop," I said. "I get it. . . . You're a superhero who can summon an army of mice with your little guitar."

"Uke," Penny said. "And don't call me a superhero. You'll get me in trouble."

"Sorry." I wasn't sure why I was apologizing. *Superhero* wasn't a bad word.

One of the teachers took the stage and tapped on the mic. Loud thumps came from the speakers, echoing through the mountains.

". . . probably start an avalanche like that," the teacher said, pulling the mic closer to his mouth. "Good evening, students of Kepler Academy! To all the sixth graders out there—I am Vice Principal Raymond Archer. Hello and welcome!"

Students clustered in front of the stage as the vice principal went on with the usual "we're gonna have a great year," and "let's learn a lot," and "seize the day!" phrases bundled into a motivational speech.

It was almost like I was at a normal school.

When the vice principal finished, he held the mic out sideways and dropped it onto the stage. When the mic hit the floor, fireworks exploded above him.

Huge domes of light popped against the dark blue sky as trails of sparks cackled loudly. I couldn't help but laugh as Vice Principal Archer danced like a magician onstage, pointing at different spots in the sky where the fireworks were going off.

The fireworks were coming from *him*.

Everyone cheered.

I was definitely *not* at a normal school.

CHAPTER ELEVEN

6 a.m.

Thursday.

The first day of school.

I was up early. Or actually, I was up all night, too excited to sleep. Or was I too *worried* to sleep? I couldn't be tardy for the first day of my origin story!

I thought Kepler Academy would have a dress code, but it didn't. Students were allowed to wear whatever they wanted. It helped make things feel normal, I think.

My schedule wasn't anything special, which was a bummer. My classes were the same ones I would've had back home. Maybe the academy didn't want dumb superheroes.

The one class that stood out was Powers & Ethics, but that was only on Saturday mornings. I wasn't sure if I could wait a whole *week* for that one.

The halls filled with students. It was easy to tell

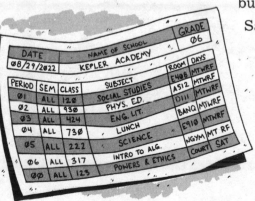

DATE	NAME OF SCHOOL			GRADE 06	
08/29/2022	KEPLER ACADEMY				
PERIOD	SEM	CLASS	SUBJECT	ROOM	DAYS
01	ALL	120	SOCIAL STUDIES	E408	MTWRF
02	ALL	930	PHYS. ED.	A512	MTWRF
03	ALL	424	ENG. LIT.	D11	MTWRF
04	ALL	730	LUNCH	BANQ	MTWRF
05	ALL	222	SCIENCE	E910	MTWRF
06	ALL	317	INTRO TO ALG.	NGYM	MT RF
00	ALL	123	POWERS & ETHICS	COURT	SAT

who was returning to the academy, because they were with full groups of friends.

When we got to our first class, Noah went through the door before me. I took a second to savor the moment.

I was officially a student at Kepler Academy.

I was so happy to be there that almost *nothing* could bring me down. . . .

Just then, a familiar voice shouted at me from inside the room.

OHHHH! LOOK WHAT THE DORK DRAGGED IN! BEN DOVER!

Sitting in the last seat of the last row was my worst nightmare.

The boy from my street.

The one who had turned me into a human Push-Up.

Dexter Dunn.

I stood in the doorway as my brain frantically connected the dots.

Of course Dexter would be at the academy. Why was I surprised? He had a superpower.

"You know that guy?" Noah asked.

"We live on the same street," I said.

"Huh. What about the other kid?"

Other kid? I was too busy making an escape plan in my head to notice Dexter joking with the kid next to him.

The other boy looked like he was trying to bring goth

back. His guyliner eyes stared at me from under a wave of purple and black hair. His skin was pale, but it *might've* been makeup. And he was levitating a spinning baseball above the palm of his hand.

VIC VICARS

"Take a picture, it'll last longer," Goth-boy said.

"Weak," I shot back. "That was like a sugar-free burn."

Being the last ones to class guaranteed that Noah and I would get front-row seats. We took the ones closest to the teacher's desk.

I slid my backpack under my chair. When I sat up, pain shot through my head as something nailed it.

A baseball dropped to the floor and rolled past my feet as Dexter and his friend snorted like horses from the back of the room.

They were the only two laughing. Everyone else was dead silent.

I spun in my seat, but before I could say anything, a chubby man huffed and puffed his way into the room.

"No powers, Vic Vicars!" he wheezed, walking quickly to the front of the class. "That goes for *all* of you. Absolutely no powers in *any* class except for Powers & Ethics."

"Vic is *such* a villain name," I whispered to Noah.

The teacher leaned against his desk to catch his breath, his green plaid vest rising and falling. His thick-rimmed glasses sat under his bushy eyebrows, which sat under his bad comb-over.

"I'm Mr. Riley, and this is social studies. But because of Vic, it's also the perfect time to remind you that powers are *never* to be used outside the designated area in the courtyard and *never* without proper supervision."

There was a grumble from the class.

Mr. Riley arched an eyebrow. "I'm not going to sugarcoat this, because it's *that* important: Uncontrolled powers can be deadly. You're all new here, but it won't take long for the horror stories of past students to reach your ears."

The pudgy teacher folded his arms and sighed. "Powers *aren't* a blessing . . . they're a *curse*."

CHAPTER TWELVE

Noon.

Later that day.

Noah and I caught up with Penny in the banquet hall during lunch. Trays of food, served buffet-style, lined one side of the room.

Penny pointed at different entrees and questioned the lunch lady. "And that?"

"Ham casserole," the lunch lady said. "Just have some salad. You'll have to pick out the bacon crumbs first."

". . . okeydoke," Penny said. "Now we're talkin'."

We found an empty table at the front of the room, next to the club sign-ups, where dozens of kids huddled together.

"What're you guys signing up for?" Penny asked, holding a cube of carrot cake in her fingers. Five other cubes sat on her tray.

"Wearable Tech sounds pretty wizard," Noah said.

"Stop saying things are 'wizard!' Just say they're cool!" Penny said. She turned to me. "What about you?"

Noah answered for me. "Definitely not the insect club, amirite? Too many spiders for this Braver kid."

"Dude," I said, shaking my head ever so slightly at my roommate. "Don't embarrass me. . . ."

"What's wrong with spiders?" Penny asked.

"Ben's *sooooper* scared of them," Noah said.

"That was supposed to be a secret!" I said, pushing my tray away. I leaned back in my seat so I could see the club names on printed sheets of paper taped to the walls. "I think kung fu is callin' my name. Besides, if I'm training to be a superhero, I should probably know how to defend myself, right?"

Noah laughed nervously. ". . . right."

"Whatever," I said, poking at my ham casserole. "What if I have to fight a giant spider someday?"

"A spider probably won't fight you with kung fu," Penny murmured.

Man . . . *how cool would that be?*

"What's the deal with this place?" I said. "I thought there'd be flying kids and explosions pretty much 24/7. Instead of training with lasers, we get a normal gym class, where we spent most of the time walking in circles around the basketball court. This is like summer camp, but *without* the deadly shenanigans."

"Uh, yeah, so it's like a real school," Penny said, white frosting on the edges of her mouth. "I get it, though. It's a little boring."

"But that's my point! This *isn't* a real school, right? At least it *shouldn't* be. I mean, everything's just so *boring*. Even the vending machine is boring! It's just a bunch of fruity, oaty things! Whose chalkboard do I gotta erase to get a peanut butter cup around here?"

Noah swallowed his bite and leaned closer. "If all you want is candy . . . I can getcha candy. The good kind, too. The kind that causes cavities and nightmares."

I covered my mouth and talked softly like we were about to make a secret deal. "Don't mess with me, dude. If you're promising peanut butter cups but don't deliver, then you'd better sleep with one eye open because I will *paint* your face like the lying clown you are."

Penny coughed out a laugh, spitting carrot cake all over her tray.

Noah looked me dead in the eye. "Follow me."

Noah took Penny and me back to our dorm to show us his secret stash.

"My mom packed it for me as a surprise," Noah said, locking the front door. "She's cool like that."

Penny fell into the old couch like she was about to die. "Stomach . . . wrecked . . . too much cake . . ."

"I owe you, man," I said to Noah, sitting on the edge of my bed. "But please tell me you've got peanut butter cups."

Noah slid open his top dresser drawer and pushed his clothes around. "Uh, I'm pretty sure I do. . . ."

Noah pulled clothes out and tossed them over his head. "It's not here! Everything's gone!"

Penny sat up. "What? Someone stole all your candy? Am I gonna see some action now?"

Noah slammed the drawer shut. "My mom packed that for *me*."

"It's cool," I said. "We'll figure it out. At least it was just candy and not—"

Penny sneezed, cutting me off.

"Gesundheit!" I said.

"That wasn't me," Penny said, confused. She pointed at Noah. "I thought it was you."

Noah shook his head. "Nope . . ."

"Who sneezed?" I asked.

Our eyes darted around the room, but no one else was there. It was just the three of us staring at each other with wide eyes.

Before we could say anything else, the bell rang. Lunch was over, and we had five minutes to get to our next class.

CHAPTER THIRTEEN

After school.

Noah and I were in the courtyard kicking a soccer ball back and forth. Nobody handed out homework on the first day of class, so we didn't really have anything else to do.

Penny sat in the grass, furiously tapping at her cell phone, playing a game or something. Her uke was by her side.

"What about that sneeze? That was probably just someone in the hall, right? Or maybe it came from the hole in our ceiling. Penny, do you have a roommate?"

"Nope, I'm all alone and couldn't be happier," Penny said.

"That doesn't mean someone *wasn't* in there," Noah said. "Maybe whoever snagged my candy was in *your* room."

"Yeah, that'll help me sleep good tonight," Penny said. "I'm totes sleeping next to that hole, so if I scream, you guys'll know. Aaaand now I'm wondering if it was a ghost we heard. Awesome."

"Do ghosts sneeze?" Noah asked.

"I dunno," Penny said. "I wanna say . . . yes? But I'm no expert in the paranormal."

"You know what's ironic?" I said. "That I'm at a school for kids with superpowers, but the most exciting part of my day was a random sneeze. It was probably the most normal school day ever in the history of all days . . . ever."

"What'd you expect?" Noah asked. "Holographic training rooms? Costume Design 101? Intro to Origin Stories?"

"Uh . . . yes," I said. "*Exactly* that. I didn't think I'd become a superhero on the first day, but I thought I'd at least be on the path. You know what I learned today? The definition of an integer . . ."

"What's an integer?" Penny asked.

"I don't know. I wasn't paying attention."

"Why'd you expect this place to be any different?" Noah asked. "Didn't your parents ever tell you about the school when you were growing up?"

I set my foot on top of the soccer ball. "Um . . . yeah, duh . . . but also, no, they didn't. I didn't even know this school existed until four days ago."

Penny looked up from her phone. "What about when your mom or dad went here? What about their powers?"

I was confused as heck. "What? My parents don't have powers. Unless you consider nagging a power! Am I right?" I said, holding my hand up for a high five that never came. "No? Nothing?"

They both gawked.

STOP LOOKING AT ME LIKE THAT... YOU'RE MAKING IT WEIRD.

A woman's voice came from behind. "I think they're a little confused about how you're at the academy to begin with."

It was the woman from the welcome ceremony—the one who craved bacon-wrapped dates. She was older—probably in her sixties. Maybe *late* sixties. I don't know—she looked like she could've been my grandma. Her fashion sense had been plucked right out of a 1950s sci-fi movie, with a v-neck hourglass dress that cinched tightly around her waist. She was wearing gloves and looked like she had been gardening.

She took my hand and shook it. "You must be Benjamin Braver. I'm Abigail Cutter, head of school security. It is *such* a pleasure to meet you."

Her grip was fierce. "You know who I am?"

"Of course I do! Everyone on staff has been talking about you nonstop!" Abigail said, her eyes shining. "You're the first student at Kepler Academy who *isn't* a descendant of the Seven Keys."

"Seriously?" Penny gasped.

Noah's jaw nearly fell off.

"Okaaay," I said, uncomfortable. "Now it's *weirder*."

Abigail laughed. "They're shocked because they know something you, apparently, don't."

"And what's that?"

CHAPTER FOURTEEN

Nothing makes you feel unwanted more than someone telling you that you shouldn't be around.

"You're not a descendant of the Seven Keys?" Noah asked.

I was on the spot. I hated being on the spot.

"You *do* know who the Seven Keys are, don't you?" Penny said.

"Yes, they're those dwarves, right?" I said.

"OMYGOSH!" Penny said.

"What are the Seven Keys?" I asked.

"I'm a bit surprised that Donald didn't explain this already," Abigail said, taking a seat on the bench next to us. "The Seven Keys—seven people. Back in 1943, those seven individuals underwent an experiment to make them superhuman, or supersoldiers."

"Because they were the first superpowered people?" I asked.

"No," Penny said.

"Was Kepler one of them?"

"No! If you'd close your mouth and let the woman talk, then you'd get your answers!" Penny said, frustrated.

Abigail continued. "Donald Kepler was a scientist who experimented on himself *before* working with the seven. His talents developed—theirs did not. Instead, their DNA unlocked talents in their children. That's why they're called the 'Keys.' Fourteen children between seven families. *I* was one of the fourteen."

"What's your power?" I asked immediately.

Abigail laughed. "I have the ability to speed the growth of plants." She stretched her arms out. "I maintain the delicious landscape of botanical specimens around the academy. It was Donald who helped me reach my full potential."

"What was the school like back then?" Noah asked.

Abigail's eyes softened as she reminisced. "The first class . . . *those* days were exciting. Donald already had his talent, which is why he took us under his wing. He started the academy to keep us secret and safe from the world. It was a private place for us to learn to control our new abilities. Part training facility, part middle school. With only fourteen students, life was simpler back then."

Noah and Penny nodded like they had heard the story before.

"You guys were all the same age?" I asked.

"We were *around* the same age," Abigail said. "The younger looked up to the older. The older mentored the younger. Back then, Donald taught the classes himself and personally helped each student with their talents."

"And then what?"

"And then? Nothing. At least not until we had children of our own. Every descendant of the Keys has developed a talent. But you . . ." she said, wagging her finger toward me. "You *aren't* related to *any* of them."

". . . Mr. Kepler asked me to come personally," I said.

"And *that's* what's exciting," Abigail said with clear eyes. "He's a wise old man. *Strange*, but wise. Doesn't do *anything* on accident. If he chose you to be here, it means you *will* develop a talent, and we're all so eager to see what that looks like. You could be the turning point of humanity—some kind of *eighth* key."

Shivers. Down m'spine.

"But with so many descendants of the Keys, that means there *have* to be superheroes living in the world, right?" I asked.

"Not superheroes," Abigail said. "Normal people with special abilities. This isn't a movie. This is the real world, where people with powers are scary. The academy is about *controlling* those powers and keeping them dormant. Not about making them stronger. Can you imagine a bad guy with real, *actual* powers?"

I could, and it was awesome.

The dinner bell rang, and Abigail said good-bye.

The day was long and disappointing, but Abigail lit a candle of hope. Kepler didn't do things on accident. He *wanted* me to be there.

Ben Braver wasn't brought in to keep things dormant.

Ben Braver was brought in to shake things up. Ben Braver thinks it's weird to be talking about himself in the third person.

I don't know what Kepler saw in me, but he saw *something*.

Something special.

Something that would make me . . . remarkable.

Kepler made me a deal to send me home at the end of the semester if I was unhappy, but the deal went the other way, too: I'd get sent home if I didn't have a power.

Back on my roof, he said I had until Christmas to discover my power. That gave me about four months.

The clock was ticking, and I didn't want to let him down.

CHAPTER FIFTEEN

The running sink in my bathroom woke me up, but when I looked inside, no one was there. It must've been in my head.

I stood in front of the mirror in my flying-pig jammies. Half asleep, I grabbed my toothbrush, which was somehow already wet with suds on the bristles.

I turned to Noah. "Dude, did you use my toothbrush?"

He rolled over, still snoring in his bed.

The cap was off the toothpaste. Water dripped from the edge of the sink down to the drain, which burped a minty white froth.

Someone had just brushed their teeth.

The running water *wasn't* in my head.

First, gross.

Second, *gross* gross.

Slowly, I turned and scanned the room.

Eerie silence.

Just then, the front door swung open and slammed shut.

Noah shot up in his bed. "Okay, I'm up!"

I bolted for the door. Whoever had used my toothbrush had to be the same person who stole Noah's candy, or more important, the peanut butter cup Noah had promised me.

But I was too late. The hallway was empty.

Something strange was going on.

There was either a sneaky thief loose in the school or a ghost with good dental hygiene. Either way, I knew I needed to find out.

I turned the handle to go back into my room, but the door didn't budge. I was locked out. And I was still in my jammies! The short shorts and tank with the flying pigs!

"Noah, let me in!" I whispered, tapping on the door rapidly.

I stood there for twenty minutes before Noah let me back in. Twenty minutes of embarrassment that I'd remember for the rest of my life.

The hushed whispers. The giggles. The cell phone camera clicks.

All ingredients for a supervillain soufflé.

Good thing I was stronger than that.

. . . I think.

An hour later, all the sixth graders were in the court-yard for class. It was the first day of Powers & Ethics, and I was ready to party.

After telling Noah about the toothbrush incident, he agreed to help me catch the ghost of Kepler Academy.

We tried telling Penny what happened, but I don't think she understood. Her eyes were open, but nobody was home.

"I was up all night playing online," she said. "Not sure I even slept. The Internet speed at this school is *redic*."

"We know," Noah said. "We could hear you shouting through the hole."

"*Oh-noessss*, you mean the hole *you* made? If you don't like it, shove a towel in it."

Like any school, students clustered with friends they made during the first week. Dexter and Vic were under a tree by themselves.

Noah and I sat in a circle with Penny and a dozen other kids.

We listened as they listed their powers one after another.

"I absorb allergies of nearby people," a boy named Arnold shared. "The allergies go away after a while."

ARNOLD   ROSE   GEORGE   TOBY   JOEL   DEVIN

"My name is Rose, and when I get soaked, my body divides in half, like there's two versions of me, but also half the size. I'll keep dividing and shrinking, too, if I don't dry up."

"George, and . . . I'm turning into a wolf. Go me."

"I'm Toby, and I got stretchy powers. Except . . . only in my big toes. They can get really long, too! Like, *stupid* long. I just discovered my power last night."

"My name's Joel, and I can open portals to travel long distances, but the portals are only about the size of a quarter. So if you need to push a tiny button that's *really* far away, I'm your guy."

"Devin. I have superstrength, and I'm bulletproof, but only for a second. Don't ask me how I learned I was bulletproof. I don't like talking about it. . . ."

A boy wearing a gas mask spoke next. "Ethan" was all he said.

"My name is Mae, and I can travel through glass. Like, I can go in at one spot and then come out at another."

One kid was buckled into a wheelchair. "So I'm

ETHAN MAE RONNIE NOAH PENNY ME

Ronnie. I repel gravity. If I get out of my seat, I'll shoot right into outer space . . . I think. I've never tried."

Noah and Penny shared next.

I was the only one in our circle who didn't have a power yet.

"Everybody, listen up!" a man's voice boomed from the side of the courtyard. "Fall in line, and we'll get started!"

All the students jogged to form a single-file line in front of the teacher.

He was a tiny guy. Short and thin. Balding, but only on top. The hair that hadn't abandoned the sides and back of his head yet was long and ragged, like he was sporting a reverse Mohawk. A whistle hung from the side of his mouth.

Dainty would be how I described him if you asked me to choose one word.

"The name's Lindsay Andrews," he said, whistle clenched firmly in his teeth. "Call me Coach Lindsay. But if you so much as *giggle* when you do, you'll find yourself doin' push-ups till your arms *literally* fall off. *Got it?*"

Someone shouted, "Sir, yes, sir!"

The rest of the class groaned.

Dexter rolled his eyes. "Looks like *you're* the one who needs to do push-ups."

"Don't judge a book by its cover, especially at this school," the coach said. "I might not look like much, but I can toss a city bus like a softball." His eyes looked past everyone, and his voice got shaky. "Twin sister used to be able to do the same."

Everyone stood uncomfortably quiet.

Coach Lindsay continued. "Each and every one of you believes you won some kind of genetic lottery, but it's *my* job to let you know thatcha didn't. You're among the most unlucky human beings on this planet."

I didn't like where this was going.

"The purpose of Kepler Academy," Coach Lindsay said, "is to learn how to control your talents so that *you never use them*. The number one rule here at the academy: No powers outside of class. Rule number two? *No powers outside of class*. Got it?"

Nobody said anything that time.

The coach paced as he went on. "Here's the ethics part of the lesson—creating humans with powers was *ethically* bad. The world would turn on us if they knew we existed. But what's more likely is that some of us would turn on the world."

"Classic villain scenario," I whispered to Noah.

Coach Lindsay stopped. "Something you'd like to add, Braver?"

Of course he already knew who I was. "I'm just saying, um . . . you're talking about supervillains and stuff."

"This isn't a comic book," Coach Lindsay said. "But you're not wrong. I've seen students with impossible talents. Once saw a kid turn into a giant snake. Attacked the school. Didn't end well. Kepler Academy exists to prevent that. No supervillains."

My heart tore in half. "But then the school exists to prevent super*heroes*, too."

"This guy's got it," Coach said, emotionless. "You're not here to learn how to create a bigger fireball. . . . You're here to learn how to keep the fireball hidden. Forever. If I catch *anyone* fanning the flame of becoming a superhero, we're gonna have problems. No costumes. No code names. No problems."

Everything I thought about the school was flipped upside down.

". . . I don't get it," I accidentally said aloud.

"Good thing you weren't brought here to *get* it," Coach said, annoyed.

I kept my mouth shut after that.

The coach gave us the rest of the afternoon to focus on our individual powers. He reminded everyone that powers were allowed only during *his* class, and also right after school as long as it was in the courtyard—and even then, under proper supervision and only for students who hadn't discovered theirs yet.

Like me.

CHAPTER SIXTEEN

8 p.m.

Later that day.

My friends and I were planted on the leather chairs outside the café. The lobby swarmed with students talking and laughing.

Noah flipped through a comic that I had brought from home as Penny practiced chords on her uke.

"So you think this ghost stole Noah's candy," Penny said, "and then brushed his teeth? That's one responsible ghost."

"Noah was still asleep when I woke up," I said. "So I know it wasn't him."

"Uh, plus I *told* you it wasn't me," Noah said.

"Just sayin'."

"So how do we catch a ghost?" Penny said.

"We could get some proton packs," Noah said. "If proton packs were real . . ."

"The ghost likes candy," I said. "We could lure it out with that."

"It also likes good dental hygiene," Penny said sarcastically. "So we'll set out a plate of candy with a toothbrush! Do you know how stupid that sounds?"

"It's not stupid if it works!" I said.

"Let's hope it works then," Noah said.

At that moment, the exit door on the side of the lobby flew open and banged against the wall. Abigail, head of school security, stormed through with a cutthroat look in her eyes. Her dress was torn and covered in dirt and pine needles like she had just fallen out of a tree.

She was seriously hurt.

"Are you okay?" I asked as she passed the coffee shop.

Abigail stopped in place. She didn't look at us as she spoke. "I'm fine. I was chasing after a student who used his powers outside. I lost him after he ran into the forest."

"Was it a ghost?" I asked.

"*What?*" Abigail snipped. "*No*, it wasn't a ghost! It was just a kid!"

"Do you need any help?" Noah asked.

But Abigail didn't say anything else. She was already on her way out of the lobby.

CHAPTER SEVENTEEN

7:30 p.m.
Sunday.

There was a ghost to find, but I also had powers to discover.

Noah and I were in our dorm. Penny was talking to us through the hole in our ceiling. The TV was on, but nobody was watching.

"More kids discovered their powers since school started," Noah said.

"I know," I said. "I can't be the last one to figure it out."

"It's not like anybody cares," Penny said. "Everyone here is too focused on their own power to see anything outside their own little bubble. *Aliens* could invade, and they wouldn't even notice."

"No such thing," Noah said.

Penny snickered. "Says the guy who breathes fire, and, oh yeah, who's also trying to catch a ghost."

Noah smiled. "Touché, Penelope, touché." He turned to me. "Maybe you need to do something to bring the powers out."

A light flipped on in my brain.

"You're right!" I said. "Superpowers don't just *hap-pen* to couch potatoes. They happen to people under pressure!"

Noah agreed with a nod.

"In comics, powers always come out as a defense mechanism when there's danger. Like, someone is about to die until their power suddenly shows up. I just need to put myself under a ton of stress!"

"Well, I think there's a senior who's turning into a dinosaur," Penny said. "He's, like, twelve feet tall already. He could sit on you."

"No, not actually *under* something," I said. "I mean, like, stress that's life-threatening. The danger's gotta be real." I turned to Noah. "I need you to slap me."

"Wait!" Penny's face disappeared from the hole. Her footsteps thumped across the ceiling, and then her door slammed shut.

Noah and I looked at each other, not sure what to do.

There was a small knock at our door.

Noah opened it.

"I wanna watch you slap Ben," Penny said, leaning on the doorframe, catching her breath. She even had a bag of popcorn. "Okay . . . go."

"I'm not slapping Ben," Noah said.

"*C'mon!*" Penny said. "I ran all the way down here!"

"No!"

"Fine," I said. "I'll just slap myself."

"Oh, yesss!" Penny said, pushing Noah aside as she invited herself in.

My friends watched as I raised my hand, took a deep breath, and slapped my own face.

"That's it?" Penny said. "Put some *beef* into it, Braver."

"Just try something else," Noah said.

Penny grabbed a heavy textbook. "Hit yourself with this! *Please* hit yourself with this!"

"I don't know," I said, taking the book.

"Regret the things you did," Penny said. "Not the things you didn't do."

"Not sure that's good advice," Noah said.

"No," I said. "She's right."

Clutching the textbook in my hands, I squeezed my

eyes shut. And then I slammed the book against the front of my face as hard as I could.

THWACK!

Noah and Penny laughed hysterically.

Unless my power was a bruised forehead, hitting myself in the face was getting me nowhere.

Things were gonna have to get a little more dangerous.

CHAPTER EIGHTEEN

My investigation of the ghost thief was going strong. Noah wasn't the only one in the school who got robbed. Several others did, too. Mostly food and snacks.

Like me, some kids said their toothbrushes had been used. A few even said their toilets flushed on their own.

And the thing we all had in common? The ghost only hung out on the third floor. My floor.

Students on other floors of the Lodge had no idea what I was talking about. That narrowed it down a ton but still didn't give me the lead I needed to crack the case.

I would've spent the rest of the night looking for clues, but I had to get to the gymnasium.

Kung Fu Club was about to begin.

A dozen kids waited on the bleachers with me, watching the doors to see which teacher was going to lead the class.

Everyone was wearing karate outfits.

Everyone except me.

I must've missed *that* memo.

At last, a girl stepped out of the locker rooms followed by Dexter, who carried a stack of wooden boards.

"Perfect," I said under my breath.

The girl was taller than Dexter by half a foot. She was really pretty, too, and there was something familiar about her, like I had seen her before, but I couldn't figure out where.

"Welcome to Kung Fu," she said as she put her hands together and bowed. "My name's Darla, and this is my little brother Dexter."

Yes! Darla Dunn! I *did* know her!

Ohhhh, crud.

I suddenly remembered seeing Darla on my street a few years ago before she was sent away to military school. . . . But it *wasn't* military school. It was Kepler Academy.

There were *two* of them at the school.

Dexter whispered something to his sister, and then she looked at me. Her lips slowly stretched into a smirk.

Probably not a good thing.

Without warning, she planted her feet and threw a chain of punches as fast as she could while peeking at us from the corner of her eye.

Dexter, grunting like an animal, threw weird kicks of his own.

The masterpiece unfolding before me was the result of *years* of devoted training in their parents' basement.

"What is this?" someone whispered. "Are we supposed to do what they're doing?"

Nobody knew the answer.

In unison, the Dunn kids pulled their fists back to their sides and slid their feet together.

Dexter picked up a wooden board.

Right then I knew . . . Things were about to get *good*. I was about to witness a train wreck.

Darla ran at her little brother, screaming like a banshee.

She pushed her foot off the floor and snapped it

at her brother, *missing the wooden board completely.*
Dexter broke the board in half by himself but acted like
Darla did it. He threw the pieces to the ground and
stumbled backward.

Dexter's sister bent her body in half and bowed.

"Now," Darla said as she caught her breath. "I need
a volunteer."

She never broke eye contact with me as everybody
else shot their hand up.

"You," Darla said, pointing her finger at my face.

I agreed, but only because I was still trying to stress
my power out, and getting beat up by Dexter's older
sister in front of my classmates sounded pretty stressful.

"Please, join me in the dojo," Darla said as she tugged the bottom of her karate gi.

"This isn't a dojo," I said. "It's a gym. A gym-jo? A do-gym? Do-gym sounds better."

"The dojo is always with you . . . here," Darla said, jabbing her finger into my chest. "Bow to your sensei. . . ."

I didn't wanna be "that guy," but she was getting everything wrong. "Karate has a sensei. Kung fu has a sifu. You can't be both."

"I've developed a style that fuses the two," Darla said. "Now bow . . ."

It felt like I was under the bridge again.

"But you're throwing punches like a hobo," I said. "What you're doing isn't kung fu. Trust me—I've watched *tons* of kung fu movies."

"What do *you* know about kung fu?" Darla asked.

"More than you!" I said, regretting it immediately. I added a bunch of other stuff to make it sound like I was only trying to be helpful. "I mean, there's the popular ones, like Shaolin, Tai Chi, or Wing Chun. And then there's animal-style ones, like Tiger, Leopard, or Dragon."

"Yeah, I know." Darla sneered. "That's what *mine* is. A fusion of *all* of them balled into one master kung fu system. It's so epic it hurts."

"I bet you call it Dunn fu, right?"

Why did I say that? Why couldn't I keep my mouth shut?

"Or maybe it's dumb fu," I added quietly.

Whatever. I was already dead meat. Might as well own it.

"Disrespecting the sifu!" Dexter shouted. "Sensei, permission to introduce the noob to my two best friends." He paused to put both of his fists up. "The right one's Guns, and the left one's Roses!"

"Calm yourself, brother," Darla said. "Ben is just nervous. You can tell because his face is red and his forehead is sweaty. Class, this is your first lesson. Know thine enemy."

Mutual agreement came from all of the students around me.

Darla continued. "From the sweat on his chubby red face, I know that Ben is freaking out right now. He's anxious and embarrassed."

She wasn't wrong, but . . . *chubby*?

"A true master would use that weakness to get into the enemy's head. Merely talking about it is making Ben sweat even more. Now," she snarled. "Bow to your sensei."

I bowed. Big mistake.

Darla threw a kick, which I successfully blocked with my face.

I flew backward but stayed on my feet. The last thing I saw was Darla coming at me with fists of fury.

An hour later, I was in the nurse's office pressing an ice pack against my black eye. The room was small and cold, and it had a weird smell to it.

Worms or something.

Noah popped his head through the door.

"Whoa . . . what happened to your eye?" he said.

"Darla Dunn happened," I said.

"That ninth grader?"

"She's Dexter's older sister."

"There's *two* of them here?"

"That's *exactly* what I said." I turned to the nurse, who looked like she needed a nurse of her own. "Can I leave now?"

She nodded once with glazed-over eyes.

"Wait," Noah said. "Don't you need to fix his eye with your healing power or something?"

Of course the nurse had healing powers. How cool was that?

"I'm sick" was all she said. "Now go."

Noah and I didn't argue.

"Did you get into a fight with Darla?" Noah asked as we walked to our dorm. "Did she lay the SmackDown on you?"

"No, she volunteered me to spar with her during Kung Fu," I said.

"*She* volunteered *you*?"

"Yeah, but I wanted it," I confessed.

"You want girls to beat you up? You got problems, man."

"Nooooo, I wanted to stress my power out. Didn't work."

We walked up the staircase in the lobby as other kids wandered around aimlessly like sleepwalkers. This school was wearing *everybody* thin.

"You going back?" Noah said.

"To Kung Fu? Flip no! I'm done with that," I said, tossing my melted ice pack into a trash can at the top of the stairs.

"You should come to Wearable Tech!" Noah said. "We meet every other Friday after school on the roof. And it's taught by Professor Duncan!"

Noah looked at me like I was supposed to know who he was talking about.

"Oh, right," he said. "You don't know about Professor Duncan."

"What about him?"

"*Nothing* . . . only that he's a supes brilliant inventor. He created those octopus robots that helped us with our luggage when we first got here."

"No way," I said. "What happened to those things? I haven't seen them since that first day."

"They were glitchy," Noah said. "Duncan shut 'em down to work on their programming."

Wearable Tech wasn't my first choice, but if Noah liked it, then I'd probably like it, too.

Actually, any club that didn't involve getting pummeled by Darla was fine by me.

CHAPTER NINETEEN

8:30 p.m.

Thursday.

Late September.

The weather was perfect—not hot, but not cold. Like that third bowl of oatmeal or porridge or whatever that girl ate in that bear story.

What the heck is porridge, anyway?

I was in the lobby café, sippin' some hot chocolate-flavored water. They didn't use milk the way my parents did.

The coffee smell, low light, and java jazz reminded me of nights at home with them.

My chair had a few broken springs, but that only made it more comfy. Like the couch in my basement. The one I binged TV on. The one Dad refused to let Mom replace. The one Mom *pretended* she wanted to replace.

I missed home.

"There you are," Penny said, leaning over the back of my chair. Her uke hung from her shoulder. She took that thing everywhere.

Noah was with her, stick of beef jerky dangling from the side of his mouth as usual. "You been here the whole time?"

I nodded. "I just wanted to be alone."

"You're like the Pluto of people," Penny said.

"Huh?"

"Like, Pluto used to be cool, hanging out with other planets doing planet things, but then it quit being a planet. Now it just hangs out all alone, pouting like the weird kid who wants to be alone in a coffee shop."

"Pluto didn't quit," I said. "Pluto was *kicked out*. *Forced* to leave because he couldn't cut it as a planet. Or she . . . are planets boys or girls?"

"Well, you can quit pouting now that *we're* here," Penny said brightly, sinking into the chair next to me. "Plus . . . look what I can do."

Penny strummed gently on her ukulele. "Wait for it. . . ."

After a couple of seconds, two white mice scampered up the side of the coffee table in front of the chair and stood on their hind legs.

Penny's fingers danced on the neck of the uke as she plucked different strings.

One mouse hopped on top of the other, balancing perfectly.

"I could only get them to come to me before. Now I can get them to do things."

"So awesome," I said, doing my best to hide my jealousy.

While Penny played with the mice, Noah ordered a snack from the café. "One chocolate-chip muffin and a coffee, strong and sassy, please."

The clerk looked confused. He wasn't young enough to be in school, but he wasn't old enough to be a teacher. "Uh, we're not allowed to sell coffee to students."

"What? Fine. Gimme a tea. Something black."

"Students can't order tea, either . . . Really, anything caffeinated is off the menu."

"But he's got a hot chocolate!" Noah said, pointing back at me. "Chocolate's caffeinated! G'uh . . . just gimme a muffin and a juice box. Stinkin' Juice Box Superheroes over here."

The clerk fetched Noah's order and handed them over.

CAN I GET A DECAF?

CONTRARY TO POPULAR BELIEF, DECAF ALSO HAS CAFFEINE. CAN YOU JUST ORDER SOMETHING LIKE YOU'RE NOT A SIXTY-YEAR-OLD MAN?

Noah punched his straw into his juice box and sat in the chair next to Penny and me. "What're you guys gonna be for the Halloween party?"

Penny slapped

my knee. "I bet you're going as some kind of uber-nerdy costumed hero, right? I saw those drawings in your sketchbook! I can help you come up with a *much better* design."

"You saw my Sketchbook of Secret Stuff?" I play-whined. "Penny . . . *that was private.*"

"I know. You were drawing in it when I was spying on you through the hole in my floor."

"Yeah, okay, *that's* not creepy. . . . But which costume did you like best?"

"None, but I can help. I have materials if you need. I have a vegan leather jacket that's too small for me. You can use it for a cape or something. It's all shiny and stuff."

"Coach Lindsay said we'd get in trouble if we did anything *superhero*-related," I said. "Like making costumes."

"He can't stop you if you're doing it for the Halloween party," Penny said.

Noah slurped his juice box with a mouthful of muffin. "Yeah, dude. There's pictures from past Halloween parties in all the yearbooks. Everyone goes as a superhero."

The front doors of the school swung open, and Dexter walked through. His friend, Vic, followed like a little puppy.

On their way to the elevator, Dexter spotted me and changed course to the café.

"Ben *Dover*," Dexter said.

"Your mom," I said, trying to come up with a burn, but I couldn't find one fast enough. So I finished the sentence with ". . . is really pretty."

"*What're you doing?*" Penny whispered angrily. "That's even *worse* than a burn!"

"My sister cleaned the floor with you," Dexter said. "Shouldn't have pressed her buttons, man."

"I wouldn't push your sister's buttons with a ten-foot pole," I said.

"It'd be an *honor* for you to press Darla's buttons!" Dexter snarled.

"Way to make it weird, Dex," Penny said.

"You're such a lamewad, you know that?" Dexter said. "I know you don't belong here. My parents said there's

nothing special about you
or your family. None of
you are related to the
Seven Keys."

"I don't know,"
I said. "I was there
that night I got
trapped in ice.
I'm not so sure
you're the one who
did it."

There was a chill in the air.

Vic felt it, too. He flicked his hair out of his eyes and looked back to see if the front doors were still open.

"What if those ice powers came from *me*?" I said. "But Kepler made a mistake and *thought* it was you. I can't really say that it *wasn't* me."

"I'm a descendant!" Dexter cried. "And you're not!"

"But what if you were adopted?" I said.

The air turned bitter cold as Dexter's eyes disappeared—just like they had under the bridge. He cracked his fists together, shooting a blast of ice at me, but I was ready.

I rolled off the chair, barely dodging his attack. Penny grabbed the two white mice and landed safely on the floor.

Vic stood slack-jawed, too shocked to move.

Dexter pulled his fists back. They swirled with

tiny ice crystals. He swung his arm at me, letting loose another icy shot.

I somersaulted across the carpet, away from Dexter's blast, but he had already set off another one. I braced for impact.

Suddenly, Noah jumped forward and burped out a fireball that canceled out the ice blast in a burst of steam, saving me from another three-day coma.

Penny clutched her uke and strummed fast. Her two white mice ran across the floor and up Dexter's pant legs.

Dexter freaked, spinning circles and punching his own legs. The mice tumbled out unharmed.

He balled up another chunk of ice and pulled his hands back to shoot it at me, but he never had the chance.

Coach Lindsay grabbed Dexter's arms and yanked him to the floor. The ice melted instantly, dropping a bucket load of water on Dexter's head.

"*What was the number one rule, Mr. Dunn?*" Coach Lindsay shouted. "*No powers outside my class!*"

Dexter pointed at Noah and Penny. "*But what about them?*"

"All three of you just won a day in detention," Coach Lindsay said, and then he pointed at me. "You, too, Ben. I saw the whole thing. You egged Dexter on."

Donald Kepler appeared out of nowhere. It was the first time I'd even seen him at the academy.

"What's going on here?" Kepler asked.

"It's under control, Don," Coach Lindsay said. "Full-day detentions for all of them tomorrow. Some yard work oughta help them burn off all their extra energy."

Kepler didn't say anything else. He took a deep breath, nodded, and then vanished right before our eyes.

He didn't even look at me once.

CHAPTER TWENTY

8:30 a.m.
The next day.

It was just the four of us—me, Noah, Penny, and Dexter—waiting to help the groundskeeper for our day of detention.

The goat that hung around the school chewed a patch of grass nearby. Every few bites, it would pause to look at us.

Noah was playing Hacky Sack with a large, smooth stone he found in the grass.

Dexter huffed loudly. "This is child endangerment. If the groundskeeper doesn't show up soon, I'm gone."

"Child endangerment? Really?" Penny laughed.

"Yes! What if a bear comes out of the mountains? What if that goat gets all crazy and attacks us?"

The goat cocked its head at Dexter like it was offended or something. It made us all a little nervous.

Noah booted his pebble across the yard.

"I wanted a turn!" I said, jogging to get the pebble.

After searching for a minute, I found it lying in a patch of dying flowers.

The gorgeous landscape that had greeted me on my first day wasn't so gorgeous anymore. The bright green leaves were darker and wilting.

The bell rang. School was starting, and still no groundskeeper.

Dexter stood, brushing off his shorts. "Welp, I'm gonna take a nap. Later, noobs."

"You can't just leave," Penny said.

"It's the groundskeeper's fault for not showing up," Dexter said as he walked away, but he didn't get far.

"Get back here right now!" a voice shouted from somewhere near the goat.

Dexter stopped and looked, but the school yard was bare except for the goat hobbling toward us.

A voice from nowhere? Was the ghost of Kepler Academy back?

"Whatevs," Dexter said. "I'm gone."

The voice spoke again, but this time from right in front of me. "Where d'ya think you're goin'? I own you for the day!"

All four of us stared at the goat, which was in the middle of our circle . . . er, square.

"Did he just . . . ?" Noah trailed off.

The goat nodded, and then it blew our minds by continuing. "I'm Totes. Totes the Goat."

"Oh. My. *Goat!*" I squealed.

The goat laughed. "*MEH-EH-EH-EH!* I graduated last year. I'm eighteen. A boy, and I wasn't created by a scientist. Not every descendant developed *useful* talents."

"Being a goat is your power?" Noah said. "That's super wizard."

Penny rolled her eyes.

"It's a genetic anomaly, like everyone else, except mine turned me into this," Totes said as he studied the statue of the boy and the snake. "Trust me, I'd rather be a *goat* than be *this* kid."

"What do you mean?" I said. "What happened to him?"

"*This* happened to him," Totes said. "This is Brock Blackwood. Brock's talent was that he could turn parts of his body into stone."

"What about the snake?"

"That giant mutant snake attacked the school one day. Brock stopped it by turnin' it to stone. Turned himself to stone, too. Ain't turned back since."

"So that's not just a statue?" Penny gasped.

Totes shook his goat head sadly. "Might be dead; might not be. Mr. Kepler's hopeful that Brock'll figure it out someday. Hopes he'll come back to us, but until then . . . he's just a nice lawn decoration."

I was beginning to see how kids and superpowers didn't mix well together.

CHAPTER TWENTY-ONE

Midnight.
One week later.

I peeked into the hallway from my door. Noah and I set the ghost trap right outside our room. When it showed up, I was gonna burst out there like a wisdom tooth tearing through some gums.

"This isn't going to work," Penny said. "You're dumb."

"What're you talkin' about?" I said. "It's *totally* gonna work! It's the best bait ever!"

"That's not bait!" Penny exclaimed, pointing through my door. "It's a spoonful of Easy Cheese!"

"Uh, first, it's a *whole can* of Easy Cheese. And second, who *wouldn't* want that?" I asked rhetorically.

"*Me,*" Penny said, unrhetorically. "*Me* wouldn't want that."

"Do you have to pooh-pooh all over this?" I said, frustrated. "If you had a better idea, then we'd be using that, but you didn't, so we're not!"

IS YOUR POWER HURTING MY FEELINGS? BECAUSE IT'S WEAK. YOU NEED TO WORK ON IT.

"Wait!" I said, glancing back at my brilliant trap. The plate in the hall was empty, licked clean. "The cheese! It ate the cheese, and I missed it! *Flippin' eggs!*"

I threw open my door and jumped out, hoping to see the ghost, but instead . . . I saw Dexter.

He turned around, his cheeks covered in cheese.

"*What?*" he said, making a face like he'd just got caught red-handed.

Probably because he had *just got caught red-handed.*

"*Is it the ghost?*" Penny asked from behind my door.

"No," I said, disappointed.

Dexter's eyes narrowed. "You got a girl in there? No girls past curfew, y'know."

"No, whatever, dude," I said. "No girls in there. I was just . . . Did you eat my cheese?"

Dexter looked down at the empty plate. "Free cheese is free cheese."

Made sense. Dexter seemed like the kinda kid who stood in front of the sample tray at a grocery store, eating until every last bit of food was gone.

"You could've at least saved some for your roommate," I said sarcastically.

"I don't have a roommate," Dexter said smugly. "He never showed up. Lucky me."

I went back into my room and slammed the door shut.

"This is a total waste of time," Penny said. "Can we just quit already? We were staring at that cheese for over two hours."

Penny was right. It *was* a waste of time, especially since Dexter ate all our bait.

Frustrated, I got up and smacked the empty can of Easy Cheese across the room.

But it never made it across the room.

The can zoomed over the couch, then changed directions instantly, like it hit something invisible.

"Ouch!" a voice shouted.

We froze, staring at the empty couch.

"It's in here!" Noah mouthed at Penny and me.

"No duh," Penny mouthed back.

My eyes went from the couch to the floor, where I saw a set of footprints pressed into the carpet. The toes . . . were wiggling.

Without hesitating, I snatched the sheets off my bed and tossed them over the couch. They rose into the air, hovering over the carpet.

Everyone screamed, including our mystery guest, who made a break for the door.

Penny and Noah dove out of the way as I chased it into the hall. I made a diving tackle but missed. My fingers slid against the sheets, but it was too fast and too far.

The sheet flew down the hallway, and then it popped into the air. It quietly drifted to the ground. The ghost got away.

But what kind of ghost eats candy, leaves footprints, and yells "ouch" when getting nailed with an empty can of Easy Cheese?

The kind that's not a ghost at all. . . . The kind that's probably *an invisible kid.*

CHAPTER TWENTY-TWO

Lunch.

A few weeks later.

Mid-October.

The air was crisp, and the cold was biting. Leaves were orange but hadn't fallen off the trees yet.

The stone snake around Brock the Statue made a nice bench for me to eat lunch alone. It was my "me-time" bench.

I've never loved deli meat, but the ham sandwiches at Kepler Academy were amazeballs.

"I bet you wish you could eat some of this, huh?" I said to Brock.

He didn't answer.

"At least you won't get the flu that's going around. It

makes kids stink." I laughed. "Penny's grossed out because her whole floor smells like germs.

". . . I yelled at her a couple of weeks ago. It was stupid. My Easy Cheese plan was dumb, and she was right. I think I was just embarrassed. I've been trying so hard to bring my power out, but it's just fail after fail after fail . . ."

I chewed slowly, watching the clouds move in the sky. "Y'know, this school isn't what I thought it was gonna be. It's *actually* kind of lame. I thought I'd be handed a superpower, but instead, they handed me homework. Gross, right?"

I looked at the stone boy.

"We're supposed to figure out what our power is on our own. Kepler's gonna send me home if I don't figure it out by Christmas."

I checked again to make sure we were alone.

"But sometimes I just wanna give up and go home now," I confessed. "Quitting now sounds better than failing later. . . . It's like I'm my own worst enemy, right?"

I laughed at the thought.

Me fighting myself?

Like that would ever happen . . .

CHAPTER TWENTY-THREE

Friday

After school on the roof of the academy.

I was feeling watered down, like when the ice melts in your pop and all you have left is brown water with a hint of Dr Pepper.

I might've been juggling too much between homework, trying to find my power, the ghost investigation, and video game tournaments.

It took me almost a month to finally make it to one of Noah's Wearable Tech meetings.

We stood with six other kids in front of a crudely built shack that looked like a rickety antique shop you'd pass while driving in the desert. Little metal trinkets hung on the outside walls. Stacks of rusted contraptions sat in front of the small building.

"Don't freak out when you see Professor Duncan," Noah said.

"Why?" I asked. "What's wrong with him?"

"Nothing!"

Other students around us giggled.

The door to the stairwell swung open, and a kid with a red sweatshirt, hood pulled over his head, rushed through the group and over to the shack.

"Sorry I'm late," he said, pulling several small objects out of the pockets of his hoodie. "I was talking to Headmaster Kepler about space and time and, apparently, lost track of it myself!"

I cocked my head. *This* was Professor Duncan?!

I stood up. "Hey, Professor. My name is Ben Braver, and I'd like to be in your club."

Duncan turned around, his face hidden in the shadow of his hood. He was exactly my height. "Benjamin Braver . . . the child who's *not* a descendant of the Seven Keys. Donald must have quite a reason for telling you about his school, let alone having you attend."

"I wouldn't know. He hasn't talked to me since I got here."

"Then there must be a good reason for that, too."

"Has he said anything else about me?" I asked sheepishly.

"Not a word," Duncan said. He held his hand out. "It's *nice* to meet you, nonetheless."

I grabbed his hand without looking and squeezed. It was cold and bony.

Too bony.

I looked down to see only bright white bones.

I yanked my hand away, and then screamed like a baby when his whole arm slid out of the red sleeve. The skeleton hand wouldn't let go no matter how much I shook it.

"Get it off!" I squealed, prancing around the way my mom did when a bee landed on her back.

Duncan pulled the hood off his head with his other

hand, revealing a skull with eyeballs that stared into the depths of my soul.

Everyone in the club laughed, including Noah. He totally set me up.

"Calm down, Ben," Duncan chuckled. "May I have my arm back now?"

I shut my eyes and took a deep breath.

It was easier to look at Professor Duncan the second time.

PROFESSOR DUNCAN

"Sorry about . . . ripping your arm off," I said, feeling a bit queasy. I handed back the professor's limb.

"It's okay. Even students who know about me react in similar ways," Duncan said and then waved at Noah. "Your friend even fainted when he first saw me."

Noah shrugged.

"But . . . I don't get it," I said. "Your power is . . . being a skeleton?"

Duncan shook his skull. "No, no, no. As far as I know, my power is that I, uh . . . I can't die."

"But . . . you're a skeleton."

"Yes, my *body* can die and *has* died as you can see, but whatever it is that gives a person *life*—a soul or what-have-you—doesn't die in me."

"But . . . why are you so short?"

Professor Duncan took a seat on one of the metal contraptions in front of the shack. "As a young boy with regenerative powers, you can bet I was a bit of a show-off. One day, *twenty-five years ago*, I was a seventh grader here at the academy. I was trying to impress my friends and, sort of . . . lost all my flesh."

"Ew," I whispered. "But also *awesome*."

"Since there was nothing left to heal, my body just kept going with my bones . . . and eyeballs."

"So you died when you were in seventh grade?"

"I *wish* I died! Oh . . . *how I wish* . . ." Duncan trailed off. Then he snapped back to attention. "But, apparently, my bones can live forever, so now I'm stuck here teaching at the school since a talking skeleton would freak out everyone in the world."

"That's so messed up."

"I know it!" Duncan laughed.

After reattaching his arm, Professor Duncan took out a box of his latest inventions—tiny metal discs with microscopic pins on the back so they could stick to any surface. Stick the disc to your skin, and it switched on automatically. It was like looking at a box of sci-fi gizmos from the future.

Each disc had a different effect on the person wearing it. One made you bigger. One made you smaller. One made you move faster. One even had the ability to teleport you.

His hobby was coming up with crazy gadgets in the event of a superpowered uprising. Gadgets that normal people could use to even the playing field in case things got bad. A lot of his stuff was made from an exotic metal I'd never heard of before—something called Trutanium.

I raised my hand. "You invented all this stuff?"

"Sure did," he said.

I raised my hand again. "What's the science behind all this? The powers and stuff?"

Duncan sighed like it was a question he'd been asked a bajillion times. "That's hard to answer. There's science behind it for sure, but we understand it better as emotion. Someone can snap their fingers and create ice from the water in the air, but they don't need to understand how it happens to master the ability. That's really the reason this school exists. Coach Lindsay went over this with you, no?"

"No," I said. "I mean, yeah."

But Professor Duncan was *way* easier to talk to than Coach Lindsay. I think Noah felt the same way.

"He said we're here to learn how to hide our powers," Noah said.

Duncan paused. "The world is afraid of things they don't understand. They'll *fear* you. And because of that, they'll try to control you. And if they *can't* control you . . . they'll end you."

"But the government knows about us?" I asked.

"They do," Duncan answered.

"So why don't *they* try to control us?"

"I don't know, but thanks to Donald . . . they leave us—*all of us*—alone."

The way the professor said it was odd. Like there was more to it than he wanted to say.

Like there was a darker secret behind it.

A darker history.

One we were probably better off *not* knowing.

CHAPTER TWENTY-FOUR

The night of the Halloween party.

I was in my bathroom adding the finishing touches to my costume.

No signs of the ghost since his midnight getaway, but I was ready for round two. I kept a pouch of chalk dust hanging from my belt. My plan was to beam him with it, covering him in white dust.

Penny pounded on the bathroom door. "Let's go already! I need nachos, like, right now! I've been watching food shows all day!"

"Hey, what kind of cheese is *not* yours?" I heard Noah ask.

Penny got real quiet. "Noah, I swear . . . if you finish that joke . . ."

"*Nacho cheese!*" he said.

The bathroom door thumped as Penny hit her head against it.

My costume was so boss that I admired it one last time before opening the door. It made me look pretty.

And awesome.

Pretty awesome.

"Nice outfit," Penny said as an eyeball swung back and forth on her face.

She was a zombie.

So was Noah.

So were half the other kids in the school.

I spun in place like a model. "Thanks! I spent *tons* of time on it, and—"

Penny held her hand up. "I'm sorry. I was being sarcastic. It's not your fault, though. It's hard to emote with this much junk on my face."

"At least mine's original," I said. "I've been out here for three seconds, and I already see *two* zombies."

"Not *just* a zombie. I'm zombie *Elvis*," Noah said. "Zombies are classic Halloween costumes!"

"It's not classic; it's easy," I said.

"The superhero costume is *easy!*" Noah said. "Talk about an unoriginal hack job!"

"Take that back or you'll feel the wrath of a thousand open fists!" I said.

"Open fists? You mean you're gonna slap me?"

"A thousand times!"

"Fine, dude, relax. Agree to disagree?" Noah said, holding his fist out.

I put my palm up. "Open-fist fist bump, or as scientists call it . . . the high five."

Noah slapped my hand with his.

"But seriously," Penny said. "Your costume looks redonk."

"I know," I admitted. "Making a superhero costume is a lot harder than I thought."

The banquet hall was decked out with all kinds of creeptastic decorations. Spiderwebs covered most of the room, bats hung from the ceiling, and the floor roiled with fog as strobe lights blinked in time with the music. A giant pyramid of black and orange balloons sat at the center of it all.

Coach Lindsay stood guard by the doors under a long banner that said HAPPY HALLOWEEN.

Zombies were everywhere.

A few students weren't dressed as anything at all. I almost missed them because it looked like they were *pretending* to be zombies. They were pale and slow, and they had a wormy-sick smell.

In fact, the whole room kind of smelled like worms. You know that smell that always lingers after a thunderstorm? It was like that.

"That's all kinds of nasty," Penny said. "There's a bunch of kids like that now. They make the bathrooms smell like fried bologna."

I turned to Coach Lindsay. "What's up with them? Are they sick or something?"

Coach nodded. "There's some kind of weird bug goin'

around, but it's nothing to worry about. The nurse is looking into it."

"She was sick with the same thing," I said. "Last time I was in there, she was all . . ." I slumped my body and rolled my eyes like I was all woozy.

"It's fine, Mr. Braver," Coach Lindsay said.

Penny went off.

Once we were farther into the room, we all split up. Penny went to a group of girls she was friends with. Noah went to a *different* group of girls he didn't even know after saying he was gonna "put out the vibe." And I went straight to the snack table, which, BTW, had *no* peanut butter cups.

I poured a drink and sipped it, pinkie out, minding my own business. I looked like a superhero at teatime. Funny how you never see superheroes taking snack breaks in movies.

That's when Dexter showed up.

He reached past me to grab a drink, totes bumping into me on purpose. Red fruit punch spilled all over the table and down the front of my costume.

"Come on, man," I said, frustrated.

"Nice one, Dover. Drink much?" Dexter said, laughing as he walked away with a handful of snacks.

Everyone watched, eager for some action.

I could've gotten angry, but I didn't feel like getting beat up again.

Instead, I grabbed a stack of napkins and started sopping up the puddle of fruit punch on the table. The juice streamed off the edge into a red pool on the floor.

In the middle of the pool were two dry spots like the juice was being repelled by something.

Something invisible.

The dry spots were shaped like feet.

And the toes?

They were wiggling.

CHAPTER TWENTY-FIVE

I played it cool.

No sudden movements.

After tossing the soggy napkins into the trash, I poured another drink and stood in the spot right in front of the wiggling toes.

The ghost was behind me. I could almost *feel* his presence.

I caught Noah's and Penny's attention from across the room and waved at them to come over. They didn't get it. They both waved back but didn't move from their spots.

I was on my own.

No bigs.

Spinning around, I threw my cup of fruit punch at the ghost, but instead of hitting him . . . I hit Coach Lindsay.

He was *not* happy about it.

He scolded me over the loud music, but I was too busy looking for the invisible kid to hear what he said.

And then I saw them—wet footprints magically cutting a path across the banquet hall.

"Stop that ghost!" I screamed as I ran.

The invisible kid panicked. Students magically got knocked off their feet as the ghost barreled through them to make his escape.

A kid named Ed was so frightened that he accidentally used his power. Over our heads, dark clouds formed out of thin air and rumbled. Rain poured down as thunder rolled and lightning flashed.

I think it was Ed's way of peeing his pants.

Rose, the girl who multiplied when wet, suddenly burst like popcorn into a hundred tiny versions of herself. They scattered like little animals, hiding under tables to get away from the rain.

Water splashed against my face as I chased invisi-kid, who was much easier to spot now that he was soaked. He looked like a kid made of glass.

He hopped onto the snack tables and made a dash for the front door. I did the same, kicking trays of food out of the way as students screamed.

Toby, the boy with stretchy powers, knew what I was doing. He tore a shoe off and stretched his big toe across the room. "Grab it and zip line to catch him!"

I jumped up and wrapped my hands around the slippery toe, zipping across the room at superspeed. I would've thought it gross if it wasn't *one of the coolest things I'd ever done.*

With one hand gripped around Toby's nasty toe, I grabbed my pouch of chalk dust with my other hand and threw it at the ghost.

In a puff of white dust that instantly turned to sludge, I saw the face of the invisible kid as he crashed to the floor.

Just then, Toby's toe whipped back, sending me flying through the air to the pyramid of balloons, which *did not* break my fall.

For the grand finale, my body flopped across the wet floor until it stopped at Donald Kepler's feet.

Toby ran up to make sure I was still alive. "Sorry, man! My toe cramped up! Are you okay?!"

From the floor, the chalk-covered invisible kid laughed at the chaos we had caused.

I had found him.

It was the victory I needed.

"Yep," I said, letting my head hit the floor. "I'm okay now."

Ten minutes later, the party was over.

The loud music in the banquet hall was replaced with the sounds of humming fans blowing on the wet floors.

Students and teachers worked to clean up the mess.

The mess that was *kinda sorta* my fault.

Coach Lindsay spoke softly to Headmaster Kepler. I couldn't hear his voice, but I knew Kepler was talking because his lips were moving.

I was in a chair at the side of the room. In the seat next to me was the not-so-invisible kid. His face and shoulders were covered in a chalklike slime. The rest of his body was still invisible. He looked like a floating mannequin that had empty slots for eyes.

"That was cuh-ray-zay," he said with a laugh. "My name's Jordan. I already know you."

I shook my head and chuckled. "Because you secretly camped out in my dorm."

"You guys play video games more than anyone else on the floor! And I like watching people play."

"Thought you could get away with it, huh? Well, I caught you. Wasn't easy, but I caught you."

"Bro, I *wanted* to get caught," Jordan said.

". . . what?"

"I've been here since the first day of school. I came in the same stupid little car that everyone else did, but on my way up, my power turned me permanently invisible."

"You're a student here?"

"*Supposed* to be, but when my car dropped me off, I thought I'd have a little fun. That and the guy I was supposed to be roommates with seemed like a jerk. Some kid named Dexter Dunn."

"Huh. You made the right choice."

"So, yeah, I haven't been to a single class. It was fun . . . at first. But after a month, it got *less* fun . . . and *less* and *less* and *less* fun."

I pushed my fingers through my hair, squeezing water out. "That's why you stole food, isn't it? You were hungry! And the random toilets flushing! Ohhhh . . . it all makes sense! But you *wanted* to get caught?"

"I couldn't live off candy and do nothing forever! It's sooooo boring! At this point, I'd rather do homework."

I pointed to the part of his body that was still invisible. "You must have a lot of control over your power since you can make all your clothes invisible, too."

"Actually, I don't have *any* control over my power. That's part of my problem. I'm invisible, but I don't know how to switch it off. I haven't seen my own reflection for, like, two months."

"Man, that's a bummer," I said. "But . . . what about your clothes then? Do they reappear after you change outfits?"

Jordan looked at me with a wicked grin. "I don't know how to turn clothes invisible."

"Huh . . ." I said. And then I understood. "Wait . . . oh, gross."

THIS'LL KEEP YOUR HEAD WARM. I THINK...

Brock was a super good listener.

"... and so he was invisible the whole time!" I said, laughing. "Jordan's cool, though. He's staying with us in our dorm now."

I pulled out my sketchbook and started doodling.

"So I'm still in act 2," I said to the statue. "I'll probably be here until I bring my power out. Once that happens, then boom, on to act 3. . . . I think."

I sketched some pictures of Kepler's eyebrows.

"Headmaster Kepler is my mentor. Mentors usually die in stories. Not all the time, but *a lot* of the time."

I set down my pen and looked up at Brock.

"I really hope he doesn't die. I don't know. Maybe he's *not* my mentor. I haven't really seen him all year. He actually hasn't even talked to me since I started here, but . . . maybe that's his way of teaching me. Like, he wants me to level up by making me feel, like, all alone? By making me feel like I'm sinking? Like, I'm watching the surface of the water get darker . . . and darker . . . and da—"

My pencil snapped in half in my grip.

I didn't even know I was holding it that tight.

CHAPTER TWENTY-SEVEN

Being away from my parents on holidays was harder than I thought it would be.

I missed them. I missed the food. I missed the naps after the food. I even missed ignoring the boring football games on TV.

Noah and I were headed to breakfast when we saw a line twisting out the cafeteria doors. Penny and Jordan were in it, standing together. As always, Penny had her ukulele hung over her shoulder. They waved us over.

Jordan was still invisible, but at least we knew where he was because of his clothes.

The line snaked all the way down the hall. I had no idea why that many people were waiting until I saw the poster on the cafeteria door.

ANNUAL KEPLER ACADEMY SUPERSHOW.

It was a talent show scheduled for the last day of school before winter break. At the bottom were the words, *"Talents will be allowed for performances."*

"Get in line," Jordan said to me and Noah.

"No cutting, ya dorks!" Dexter shouted from several spots behind us.

Vic was next to him. "Get to the back of the line, Dorothy!"

"Did he just call me 'Dorothy'?" I whispered.

"We were holding their spots for them," Penny said.

"You can't do that!" Dexter said, glaring. He looked right at me. "Why are *you* even in line? You don't have a power! You're the only one here who hasn't got one yet!"

I stared at the ground. Nobody said it, but everyone thought it. I was the only one left in the school without a power.

My four-month deadline was coming up. If I didn't develop one in the next thirty days, I'd have to pack my bags and go home. The *first one ever* to go home.

Dexter shouted again. "Back of the line like everyone else!"

Penny swung her uke around and gave Dexter the evil eye.

He backed off immediately.

"Anyone else got a problem?" Penny said. Everyone went back to what they were doing. "That's what I thought."

Once we got to the sign-up table, Noah and Penny filled out papers right away. Jordan didn't. He was too cool to enter.

And without a power, I didn't bother signing up, either.

Noah and Penny dropped their slips of paper into a little bucket at the end of the table. The four of us walked out the second set of cafeteria doors into the hallway.

Just then someone bumped into me hard enough that I fell in front of everyone. It was Dexter.

"Watch where you're walking, man!" Dexter shouted. "You almost knocked me over!"

I stood, but Dexter shoved me again. "Now tell me you're sorry!"

"C'mon, man!" Noah said, putting his hand on Dexter's shoulder.

Dexter pulled away from Noah and out of nowhere lunged toward me with his fist.

I flinched, covered my face, and tried to drop to the ground. Instead, I felt a rush of air like I was being pushed up, not down.

I heard the gasps of other students around me.

"Ben!" Penny shouted.

I spread my fingers open and peeked out at every-one. They were all underneath me. *Way* underneath me.

Dexter's mouth dropped open as he stared at me, his fist still in the air. His punch never had the chance to land. I finally did the thing I'd been trying to do all year.

I had discovered my power.

I was flying.

I didn't know how, but I did it. I hovered over every-one in the hallway as they clapped their hands and cheered.

Dexter was steaming, but he didn't do anything else. Vic hid behind him, jerking his head to get his hair out of his face.

I floated closer to the carpet—somehow. Noah, Penny, and Jordan reached out to pull me the rest of the way down.

"You did it!" Noah said, wide-eyed and smiling.

My blood was pumping. I'd never felt so alive!

I threw my arms around Dexter and hugged him tightly. "Thanks, man! You helped bring my power out!"

Dexter growled as Vic pulled me off him.

I had to celebrate. I had to do *something*.

And then the poster for the talent show caught my eye.

Without another word, I ran back to the sign-up table and entered the show.

CHAPTER TWENTY-EIGHT

8 a.m.

Early December.

Saturday.

The next couple weeks dragged as I tried desperately to re-create what happened in that hallway. If I was gonna be in the talent show, I needed to learn how to fly on command, but that just wasn't happening.

I did it without thinking the first time, so what was wrong with me? At least I didn't feel out of place anymore.

While most of the students were taught to hide their power, I was given a pass. I had to first learn how to switch it on before I could learn to control it.

Early December in the Colorado mountains was like being on an ice planet. The sun was shining, but everything was frozen solid.

None of that stopped Coach Lindsay from holding class outdoors. "Builds character," he said.

Even the sick kids were outside for Powers & Ethics. They huddled together in their own separate cluster, too cold to socialize or even make eye contact with anyone else.

"Maybe I should go pick another fight with Dexter," I said, defeated.

"Or his sister," Penny said. "Can't believe *nobody* got a video of that. Like, *nobody*."

"Dude, you'll get it," Noah said. "Just keep trying."

"I've been trying for the last two weeks!" I said.

"It happened once; it'll happen again," Jordan said, steam rising from the empty space under his beanie. "Just chill and be patient."

"You should try jumping off the top of the academy," Penny suggested. "Wait, I'm joking. Knowing you, you'd actually do it."

Coach Lindsay walked up to our little huddle, his whistle hanging from his mouth. "Ben, you still having trouble with the whole flying thing?"

I nodded.

"Jordan made a good point," Lindsay said. "You might be concentrating *too* much. You've tried stress. Have you tried to relax?"

Maybe Coach Lindsay and Jordan were right.

"Close your eyes and try meditating," Lindsay said.

"You'd be surprised at what you can accomplish when you shut your face."

My friends looked at me, hopeful. I closed my eyes and concentrated on the blood vessels behind the lids.

Deep breath in.

Deep breath out.

In my mind, I floated higher and higher into the air, through the clouds, the atmosphere, and then into space. The stars twinkled like they were cheering.

My shoulders and arms felt heavy. My head tilted back as my neck muscles loosened.

I heard Penny squeak, and I knew something was happening. I kept my eyes shut, hoping to keep calm and make it last.

The whispers from other students drifted away, and finally, I opened my eyes.

I was above the trees.

Coach Lindsay slow-clapped. Noah and Penny watched in awe. Even Dexter and Vic were impressed, staring up at me from the back of the group.

I was flying again.

Boo-yah.

CHAPTER TWENTY-NINE

J ordan and I sat in the chairs outside Cool Beanz, eating buttered toast and drinking hot chocolate after a long day of school.

Anything Jordan put into his body turned invisible. Good thing, too, because watching him digest food would've been on my top-five list of grossest things ever.

Number one on that list . . . milking a cow.

"How's the flying thing goin'?" Jordan asked.

"M'eh" was all I said.

The truth was, I was too afraid to try again. I'd done it twice, both times on accident. You'd think that would motivate me and get me to try harder.

You'd think.

If anything could force me to figure it out, it would be the talent show. So that's what I was waiting for. I'd either succeed and be remarkable or I'd epically fail and get sent home.

"Hello, boys," Abigail Cutter said, appearing out of nowhere.

She looked exhausted. Her pale skin and bags under her eyes gave it away.

Her smile reminded me of my mom's.

So did her eye-bags.

"Are you feeling okay? Did you get the bug?" I asked.

She pressed her lips to the side. "I did. And it's really doing a number on the students and staff."

Even though she was sick, she didn't smell like worms. That's the difference between adults and middle schoolers—adults shower.

"Does Headmaster Kepler know what it is yet?" I said.

"He's far too busy with *other* things. This is the kind of bug that happens every year, though. Students become weary because they miss home—their immune systems grow weak—they get sick—they pass it to teachers and staff. We just need to let it run its course."

Jordan and I nodded.

"So I was hoping to get two strapping young men to help me move some stuff outside?" she said. "I happen to see two right now."

"Uh, sure," I said. "What do you need to move?"

"Some new plants I've been experimenting with. I need to clean out all the old ones. Not get rid of them . . . just put them away in storage for a short while."

"Ohhhh," Jordan said. "So that's why all the flowers around here are wilting. Because you're working on new ones."

"Exactly," Abigail said. "So if you could—"

Penny jogged into the lobby and plopped herself upside down onto one of the chairs in our circle. She let out a heavy . . .

"Okay then," Abigail said. "So I'm just going to—"

Penny sighed louder.

Jordan took the bait. "Something wrong?"

"Nooooo," Penny said softly.

Jordan and I looked at each other. At least I think he looked at me.

"Really . . . it's nothing," Penny said.

"Seriously," Jordan said. "What's up?"

"It's just . . ." Penny said, pausing. "There's this video game tourney in the library tonight that I *really* wanna play in, but . . ."

"But what?"

"It's, like, *ten* bucks to enter, and I really—"

"I got ten bucks," Jordan said, pulling a bill out of his wallet with his invisible hand. It floated in front of him.

Penny snatched it up and jogged away. "Thanks, 'kay, bye!"

"Whoa," Jordan said, still holding his wallet open. "She's good."

I turned back to Abigail, ready to help her in the courtyard, but she was already across the lobby. A few other students followed her out the doors.

"Should we go with her?" I asked Jordan.

His baseball cap shook back and forth. "She's fine. Besides, she's got that bug. I don't wanna catch it from her, do you?"

"No, you're right," I said. "But I hope she feels better soon."

CHAPTER THIRTY

The talent show was a week away.

Snow was falling. Brock was covered in the stuff. I was bundled up in my swank Kepler Academy peacoat.

"So that's what I'm really afraid of," I said aloud to my stone friend. "Everyone's gonna be watching. If I can't fly in front of them . . ."

I flipped through the pages of my sketchbook as snow landed on the thick paper.

"My friends have been *so* awesome, even though I'm pretty sure they're disappointed. They try to hide it, but they're not very good at it."

Brock was quiet.

"Like, they *have* to feel weird about hanging out with the one dude at school who just can't get it, right?" I paused, listening to the silence. "You're not disappointed in me, are you?

"I honestly don't know what I'll do if I bomb at the talent show. The worst that can happen is that I'll stand on the stage and do nothing. At least I know I *have* a power. No need to go home at the end of the semester, right?"

Brock said nothing.

"Oh, right. Sometimes I forget you're just a dead kid," I joked. "Thanks for listening, dude. Sometimes I feel like you're the only guy I can talk to."

I swear it looked like he smiled.

CHAPTER THIRTY-ONE

The talent show.

Christmas break was a day away.

It had snowed nonstop for a whole week, leaving a thick white blanket that cuddled up to the school.

Nobody was allowed to go home for the holidays— one of the cons of attending the academy. I knew that coming in, but it still bummed me out.

The winter hit everyone extra hard, spreading the flu like wildfire. Coach Lindsay said the same thing as Abigail—that it happens every year. But he also said this year was the worst he'd seen.

Half the students backed out of the talent show because of it.

My friends and I were lucky. No bug yet, probably because we spent so much time away from everyone else.

From backstage, I watched kid after kid perform for the crowd and show off their power.

Noah had already gone. He had set up twenty-six balloons and popped them all with burped-up fireballs while reciting the alphabet. He got a standing ovation.

Soon it was gonna be my turn.

Toby was up. Then Penny. Then me.

I was so nervous my lips were numb.

"You okay?" Noah asked, holding two hula hoops. He was still backstage because he was part of my act. The hula hoops were part of it, too.

"No," I said honestly. "I probably shouldn't have pregamed so much spaghetti. My stomach's startin' to hurt."

Carbo-loading. It's a thing.

"You're gonna kill it out there," Noah said.

I hoped he was right.

The auditorium roared as Toby unwrapped his performance. He was dressed like a professional boxer, using his big toe as a jump rope while he exercised to "Eye of the Tiger."

Every student who wasn't sick in their dorm was in attendance. Upperclassmen, too.

Teachers stood along the back wall of the auditorium. Abigail was standing alone near the back exit. Her arms were folded as she scanned the crowd for troublemakers. Kepler was with Vice Principal Archer and Professor Duncan, pointing and commenting on each performance. Seeing Kepler only made me more nervous.

Toby waved to the cheering crowd and walked off the stage.

The host of the talent show took the mic and introduced Penny. She sat on a stool behind him, her uke resting on her lap.

The lights dimmed. She strummed gently.

The audience grew quiet as she sang a song she wrote. A white mouse scurried to the front of the stage and *danced* to her tune.

I was mesmerized. It was the most beautiful thing I'd ever heard. I was so busy trying to unravel my own talent during the year that I hardly even noticed how much hers had grown.

PEOPLE LOVE TO HATE YOUR GUTS,
BUT I THINK YOU'RE TOTES ADORBS,
SO I WROTE THIS SONG JUST FOR YOU,
WITH THESE FOUR POWER CHORDS.

YOUR SKIN IS PINK AND WRINKLY,
YOUR FUR IS SOFT AND WHITE,
I LOVE YOUR LITTLE WHISKERS,
AND THOSE EARS? I KNOW, RIGHT?

AT THE VERY SIGHT OF YOU,
THEY'LL SCREAM AND SHOUT, "LOOK THERE!
A MOUSE, A MOUSE! DON'T YOU SEE?"
WHILE PULLING OUT THEIR HAIR.

BUT I DON'T THINK YOU'RE GROSS AT ALL,
IN FACT, I THINK YOU'RE COOL,
DON'T LISTEN TO WHAT OTHERS SAY...

Penny stopped playing abruptly. She put her lips right against the microphone, and her voice boomed over the speakers. *"Because some people are just dumb."*

Everyone laughed.

She stood and bowed. Her white mouse bowed, too. Cue the roaring applause.

I was next.

Penny walked backstage as kids continued to clap for her performance. Some were even chanting *"Encore!"*

Penny smiled deviously at me. "Good luck following *that*."

Onstage, the host spoke into the mic. "Next up, Ben Braver and his incredible magic act!"

I puked a little in my mouth.

It tasted like spaghetti.

CHAPTER THIRTY-TWO

The lights were blinding. The only seats I could see were the first two rows. Dexter and Vic sat front and center. They probably wouldn't heckle me in a crowd that big.

Probably.

Noah stood behind me with the hula hoops ready to go.

For a few seconds, everything was quiet.

The lights dimmed. Fog rolled across the stage.

It was time.

Over the speakers came the most epic song ever written.

It started with a synthesizer. Then came the electronic horns. The horns got bigger and bigger until everything dropped out, and the singer wailed, *"The finaaaal countdowwwwn!"*

That's when the beat dropped. Music pumped as colored lights above us blinked in time with the song. Noah and I went right into our dance routine as wind machines blew our billowy shirts.

Bass thumped as Noah did the Robot with his serious

face. I was spinning circles on one foot, shooting jazz hands out every few rotations.

And then, in the heat of the moment, Noah tore off his shirt.

I sat cross-legged on the ground and placed my hands on top of my knees, pressing my thumb and middle finger together.

The music played as I concentrated.

Thirty seconds passed, but with all eyes on me, it felt like an eternity.

The song repeated. *"The final countdowwwwn!"*

Still nothing!

I took a breath and focused on things that made me happy. Peanut butter cups. Swimming in the ocean. Penny Plum.

And then . . . the floor pulled away.

It was working!

The song repeated again, and I savored the moment. *"The final countdowwwwn!"*

My act was more than just flying, and I had to stay cool and remember that.

Shirtless Noah was already under me, holding the two hula hoops. I stretched myself out and imagined floating in place.

"Now?" Noah asked.

"Now," I said proudly.

"The final countdowwwn!"

Noah took the two hula hoops and passed them over my body to prove no strings were attached.

Just as the second hula hoop went over my foot, my body floated higher. Noah had to raise his arm to keep the hula hoop from touching my shoes.

"What're you doing?" he whispered, panicked.

"I don't know! I can't control myself!"

I floated higher and higher. Noah grabbed my legs and hung on tightly to keep me from floating away, but it didn't work.

The two of us were ten feet above the stage when I changed directions and floated over the audience.

"Dude, you gotta come down!" Noah said.

"I'm trying!" I said. "It's not working!"

We were in the middle of the auditorium when the room started spinning. Scratch that—*I* was the one spinning.

Noah lost his grip and fell into the chairs below as kids dove out of his way.

Everything became a blur of lights and colors and music that blared way too loudly.

"Final countdowwwwn!"

I squeezed my eyes shut as my body spun wildly over the screaming kids below. My stomach gurgled, and I knew what was about to happen. I slapped my hands over my face to keep it from happening, but it was no use because it was *already* happening.

I barfed.

Have you ever barfed while spinning in circles ten feet in the air? You know who gets hit when that happens?

Everyone.

Everyone gets hit while you're barfing and spinning in circles ten feet in the air.

The worst part was that I was still spinning when I stopped puking.

No wait, the *worst* part was when I started puking *again* after I had already stopped.

"The final countdowwwwn!"

So all the kids who were just realizing why their shirts smelled like spaghetti got hit with a second round of half-digested bright red tomato sauce and pasta.

My body jerked in midair, and I was flung into the stage curtain like I was a puppet on strings. My ability to fly was gone, and I was falling. Squeezing the red velvet in my hands, I slowed myself just enough to not "Humpty Dumpty" all over the stage.

"The final countdowwwwn!"

Why didn't someone turn off the music!?

The auditorium was like a fever dream. I had started a barfing chain reaction that went several rows back. I barfed, which made someone else barf, which made someone else barf, which made someone else barf. . . .

Kids screamed, not knowing which way to run, like they were in a horror movie. One way was life. The other way was vomit.

And the smell . . . *holy wow, the smell!*

I was on my hands and knees, center stage, with a spotlight shining on my wet face.

There in the first row sat Dexter and Vic.

The music finally stopped, and I could hear everything. The gagging students. The squeaking sneakers. Dexter and Vic talking.

"That wad thought he could fly!" Dexter laughed.

Vic waved his hand at me. Instantly, my arms pulled forward and I landed painfully on my chin.

"We had that noob going the whole time!" Dexter said.

I suddenly remembered the first day of school, when Vic used his power to levitate a baseball.

Every time I flew, Dexter and Vic had been around.

I was never flying. It was always Vic using his power to levitate me.

Those two had been playing me the whole time.

CHAPTER THIRTY-THREE

Midnight.

I was on the roof of Kepler Academy.

The talent show had been canceled, and everyone was ordered to return to their dorms to shower. Special forces were called in to clean the horrid mess in the auditorium.

The sky was extra clear. The moon was full and huge, and every star in the galaxy flickered. The city lights shimmered from the valley below.

Sitting on the roof wrapped in a blanket and staring at the stars felt familiar. It felt like I was back home, which was the only place I wanted to be at that moment.

The North Star was shining bright, but I refused to look at it.

Dad said to look at the North Star if I ever felt alone. I was more alone than ever, but too embarrassed to show my face to the star—like my dad would somehow see me through it and be disappointed.

He probably never looked at the North Star anyway. It was just something dads say to make their kids feel better, right?

Man, that thought made me fight back some tears.

A gust of wind pushed against my blanket, and without even looking, I knew Kepler was sitting beside me.

"Nice night," Kepler said—the same first words he said to me on my roof back home.

I shook my head. "*Terrible* night," I mumbled, mortified.

Kepler was quiet for a few seconds. If he was up here to make me feel better, he was failing.

I took a breath and watched the fog rise from my mouth. "This school is really tough."

"I didn't say it was going to be easy," Kepler said. "In fact, if I remember correctly, I said it was going to be excruciatingly difficult."

"You also said I wouldn't stand out at all."

Kepler sighed. "Yes, but you'll have that when vomiting on half the student body."

"I was set up," I said quietly.

Kepler nodded. "Yes, I already know about Vic and Dexter. They'll be dealt with accordingly."

"They made me think I had a power," I said, feeling my cheeks burn hot in the cold air. "But I don't. I don't have *anything* yet! At this point, I'm the only kid here without one!"

Kepler said nothing. It was frustrating.

"Why me?" I asked, tears threatening to escape from my eyes. "Why'd you even want me here? I'm not a descendant of any of the Seven Keys. . . . So why me?"

Kepler took a deep breath. "I was with you for the three days you were in a coma, Benjamin. In those three days, I saw something in you . . . something *special*. That your path at Kepler Academy would lead to greatness."

After the night I had, it felt good to hear him say that. His words were warm even in the cold air. "Then why haven't you talked to me since I got here?"

"Because your path is yours to walk alone."

I sighed. Of course, after all that time, he was gonna give me a vague answer. Everyone kept saying he did things very intentionally, but I was beginning to wonder if people were just connecting dots that weren't there.

"Has anyone else taken this long for their powers to show?" I asked, afraid of his answer.

"Benjamin," Kepler said, fixing his eyes on the stars above. "I'm sorry I have to tell you this now, but you don't have any abilities, and you *never* will."

I blinked. ". . . what?"

"Only descendants of the Seven Keys develop a talent." Kepler's voice choked as he said it. "You're not. Therefore, you won't."

My jaw dropped. I didn't know what to say.

The headmaster continued. "We made a deal on your roof before school started. Do you remember? If, by Christmas, you weren't happy *or* if you hadn't developed a talent, you would be sent home, your mind and your parents' minds wiped clean of the experience."

". . . I remember . . ."

"If you're unhappy, then there's a car waiting for you in front of the school."

There it was.

The end of my adventure.

My epic failure.

Kepler disappeared, leaving me alone on the roof.

I was wrecked.

My world was shattered.

Everything I had hoped for was gone.

All my dreams . . . destroyed.

I was alone. A thousand miles from my parents. Somewhere in the mountains of Colorado. On the roof of a school I shouldn't even know about. That I shouldn't even be attending.

The good thing about being alone is there's nobody there to see you cry.

I just wanted to be with my parents . . .

. . .

I *just* wanted to be with my parents . . .

. . .

I just wanted to be with my parents . . .

CHAPTER THIRTY-FOUR

I was sitting on the stone snake in front of the school. My backpack and two suitcases lay on the ground.

The Volkswagen Beetle was parked in the street, lights on, engine running.

I saw it, but I couldn't bring myself to get into it.

I was just sitting out there, waiting for nothing.

The pages from my sketchbook were torn out and lying in the snow in front of me.

I focused on destroying my origin-story pages. Just tearing them to shreds.

Thought it'd help me feel better.

It didn't.

"I messed up," I said to Brock.

Brock didn't say anything. The jerk.

"I thought I was special—that I was destined to be something great."

Again, nothing from the statue.

"I know, right? Like, I was gonna be the first person to develop powers who wasn't related to anyone from the Seven Keys. All semester I thought I was some kind of Chosen One . . . that I was important. Like, I was gonna be the center of everyone's attention. But I'm not. I'm not the center of anything. I'm *nothing*, and *nobody* cares.

"Coming here was a mistake. I should've stayed home and kept living my normal, stupid, boring life. Why'd Kepler even waste my time if he knew I wasn't gonna have powers? I *never* would've come if I knew that back then."

The words hurt as I said them.

"I'm just . . . *nothing*. I'll never be anything. I'm normal . . . so boringly normal."

Snow silently fell all around.

"But I bet you wish you were normal, huh?" I asked Brock. "At least you'd still be alive."

For a second I thought I saw his eye twitch.

"But I am, Benjamin!" came a loud voice from the statue. "I *am* alive!"

I slipped off the stone snake and fell flat on my butt. With gaping eyes, I stared at the statue, expecting Brock to burst free from his stone prison.

Laughter erupted as Penny, Noah, and Jordan stepped around the statue.

"No, I'm kidding," Penny said, patting Brock's shoulder. "This kid's dead. Totally. Stone-cold. Dead. You should've seen your face, though." She twisted hers and mocked me. The mouse on her shoulder mocked me, too, like an itty-bitty Penny.

Their impressions were spot on.

"Dude, are you crying?" Noah said.

I sat up, put my arms on my knees, and hid my face. "No."

"Aw, quit bein' such a sad sack!" Penny said, gently patting the top of my head. "Just shake it off and be cool. That's what I'd do."

"But you *are* cool," I said. "It's *easy* to be cool when you're already cool."

"What's with the luggage?" Noah asked.

"And did you rip up your sketchbook?" Penny asked.

"Yes," I said, pouting. "I'm going home."

My friends turned to look at the Volkswagen.

"Oh, wow," Noah said. "That's for you?"

"Mm-hmm."

After about twenty seconds, Noah broke the silence. ". . . you were going to leave without telling me?"

"Didn't think you'd care," I said. "Pretty sure I beefed it tonight."

"More like *barfed* it," Jordan said.

"Thanks," I said drily.

"But nobody cares about that," Noah said.

"*Everyone* cares about that," Penny said. "There's no way you'll ever live this down . . . unless you save the world or something."

"With what powers?" I asked.

"Dude, you *barfed* on the *whole school*," Jordan said. "How many people can say that? Sure, someone can say they got one, two kids, tops. Maybe a whole lunch table full of kids, but you . . . you got *everyone*. Tell me that's *not* a power."

"Are you trying to make me feel better?" I asked.

"It's just funny," Penny said. She reached into her pocket and pulled out a peanut butter cup. "Here. I got this for you."

I reached for the cup, but the mouse on Penny's shoulder ran down her arm and snatched it before I could. All four of us watched as the mouse dashed away with the peanut butter cup, leaving tiny little prints in the freshly fallen snow.

"You can't leave," Noah said. "You're my best friend, and the rest of my time at Kepler Academy will be *so lame* if you're not around! I promise your power will come out soon."

"Oh, right," I said. "You haven't heard the best part yet. So *I* don't have any powers at all, and I'm *never* going to get them."

"You're just bummed," Jordan said. "They'll come out by the end of the year. For sure."

"No," I said, feeling a lump in my throat. "Kepler told

me, like, an hour ago. I'm *never* gonna have powers. He said he knew it when he asked me to come to the school."

"But . . ." Penny said, "why would he do that?"

"To mess with me," I said. "Maybe he's starting a superhero sidekick program, or something. Ugh . . . I'll never break through that sidekick glass ceiling."

"Mmm." Jordan looked at Noah and Penny. "That's because a sidekick can never become better than the hero."

"I know what 'glass ceiling' means, Dumbo," Penny said.

Noah paused. "But Professor Duncan said Mr. Kepler doesn't make mistakes. Everything that man does is *so* on purpose. Did he tell you to leave?"

"He said if I was unhappy, then that car is for me."

"That's not telling you to leave," Penny said. "That's just telling you that you can if you want. Do you *want* to leave?"

"No!" I said. "But it's not like I have a choice!"

"I dunno. . . . Sounds to me like you do," Penny said. "Maybe Kepler feels bad about the whole thing and would allow you to stay for the rest of the year."

"He never said '*go home*,' right?" Noah said.

I smooshed my cold face into my hands. "Right, but then why is he being so confusing? Why didn't he just tell me to stay or go?"

"Maybe he's giving you more time," Jordan said.

"But you gotta *want* it. I mean, he sent a car for you, but he never said you *had* to leave."

My friends were right. Kepler, in a frustratingly vague way, might've been letting *me* make the choice.

"Don't get in the car!" Noah pleaded. "I know you don't want *your* memory wiped, but it kills me to think about the memory of *me* getting wiped from your brain! Like, I'll remember that we were best friends, but you wouldn't even recognize me."

I looked at Noah, Penny, and Jordan's clothes.

Those three had become my best friends.

In that moment, I knew I *couldn't* go home.

The Volkswagen was still running.

VRRRRRRRRR...

Maybe my adventure didn't have to end.

I didn't show Kepler anything special in the first semester, but maybe he was giving me the second semester to try again.

"But what do I do if I know I won't get any powers?" I asked quietly, still kind of embarrassed about it.

"You could just be a normal dude with gadgets!" Noah blurted out. "Batman and Iron Man are like that!"

Duh! Why didn't I think of that? Not all superheroes had powers. I mean, Bruce Wayne and Tony Stark were supergenius billionaires, which was kind of the opposite of me at that moment. But being a supergenius billionaire *was* on my bucket list.

"It's not the worst idea ever," I said.

"Dude," Jordan said, snapping his invisible fingers. "You know who's got tons of spare gadgets lying around, right?"

I sobered up. "Professor Duncan."

"He would *totally* help," Penny said with a smile.

"He's out of town until school starts, though," Noah said.

"And he's always talking about using advanced technology to even the odds between humans and supers," I said. "I bet he'll totally say yes!"

CHAPTER THIRTY-FIVE

"**N**ope!" Duncan said right off the bat.

Winter break was over, and I went straight to the roof before first period.

I was wearing my new winter gloves that my parents sent me for Christmas. They also sent a box of graphic novels, some cookies, and hot chocolate mix. No peanut butter cups, though.

Kepler never said anything to me about not getting in the Volkswagen. He even said hello to me the couple of times I saw him after that night, which meant my friends and I were right—he *was* allowing me to stay.

Maybe he saw something else in me.

But if I wanted to figure out what that was, I knew I had a lot of work to do, especially if my path was mine to walk alone.

I'd been camped out in my dorm ever since the "barf-heard-round-the-world" incident, too embarrassed to face anyone because of it.

Noah brought meals back to the room so we could eat in privacy. I was a total shut-in, like some guy afraid of the real world, cracking the door open only an inch to see who knocked on it.

It was freezing out, but Duncan couldn't feel it. He was wearing swim trunks and hitting golf balls off the roof of the Lodge.

"Look, Ben, I'm sorry to hear about your situation," he said, "but what you're asking me is *kind of crazy.*"

I stood behind him like a little child. "But you said all this stuff was so humanity could stand a chance in case something *bad* happened!"

Duncan swung his club, hitting another white ball into the forest below. "Uh, yeah. For if something *bad* happened. Not in case some kid had a death wish."

"I don't!" I said. "I just . . . I want to belong here so badly. . . . And after what Kepler said . . . I know that I'll *never* belong, no matter how hard I try."

"So you wanna fake it?" Duncan said.

"I mean . . ." I said, and decided to go with the truth. "Yeah. You've got all these cool gadgets I could use! Like, those metal discs that do different things when they're activated. You know, like the one that forms a bubble shield, or the other that shrinks things, or—"

"Those discs are *not* toys, Ben! They're untested and *highly* unstable!"

"Maybe I could test them," I suggested quietly.

Duncan stared at me for a moment. I couldn't tell what he was thinking because he had no face.

I thought maybe I could butter him up some. "Your skull looks nice and white today. Did you bleach it while you were on vacation?"

Duncan laughed loudly and shook his head. "I'm *not* okay with what you're asking. It's dangerous and irresponsible and just pretty stupid in general. Wearable Tech isn't about making superheroes—it's about progressing the human race with technology. And to top it off, I suppose you're asking me to keep it a secret from Donald?"

The professor stopped and took a deep breath.

Even though he didn't have any lungs.

Not sure how that worked.

"But I have to admit," Duncan said. "The whole reason I started tinkering with gadgets was because my only ability was *not* dying. I couldn't fly or shoot lasers out of my eyes or anything cool like that, so . . . I know how you feel."

"So you're telling me there's a chance," I said with an eager nod.

"You remind me a lot of myself when I was your age. I don't know if that's good or bad yet. . . ."

"But you're still saying yes?" I asked, almost giddy.

Duncan threw his arms up. "Ben, I could lose my job if I said yes! And then what? If you haven't noticed, I'm a *walking skeleton!* That means I'm *unemployable.*"

I stared at the ground, defeated.

Duncan stood there silently waiting for me to say something else.

I didn't.

"I'm sorry, *but I can't say yes*," he said, putting his golf club away. He talked over his shoulder as he headed back to the stairwell. "I better not see you on the roof trying out *any* of my gadgets from my shack that's *never* locked and is almost *always* unattended. Saying no to you just means that I'll *never* have to remind you to be *respectful* and *responsible* with each piece of gear out here, and to *never ever ever* touch anything liquid."

Was he saying what I thought he was saying?

Duncan stopped in the open door of the stairwell and looked at me. I think he could tell I was confused. "I can't *say* yes. . . ."

The door shut behind him, leaving me alone on the roof of Kepler Academy.

He was *definitely* saying what I thought he was saying.

CHAPTER THIRTY-SIX

The cafeteria.

The first day back in class was a half day that ended with an indoor picnic in the cafeteria.

My day was going about as horribly as I thought it would. Pretty sure I wasn't gonna live down what happened at the talent show.

Like, ever.

Noah, Penny, Jordan, and I sat with our grilled hot dogs and BBQ potato chips. The lunch staff prepared a vegetarian alternative for Penny. All they gave her was a pile of steamed broccoli.

"This is what they call an alternative?" Penny asked. "I bet they forgot, and this is just some teacher's lunch. They don't even care."

"Ben Barfer!" someone shouted as he passed us. It was a boy named Alex, who was usually pretty quiet. I guess he found something to be loud about.

I lowered my head. My friends said nothing.

Noah broke the silence. "This is pretty lame for a welcome-back indoor picnic."

"Indoor picnics make as much sense as farting in a space suit," I said.

Boom.

Fart joke *and* a space suit joke.

Nailed it.

"It's lame cuz everyone looks bored," Jordan said. "Half these kids look like they're sleepwalking. They're all slimy looking." Jordan set his food down and looked at a boy sitting at the end of our table. *"Take a shower, Greg!* And . . . are you *licking* your bread!?"

Greg licked his bread again.

"Sick," Jordan said. "This room *stinks* like hot dog water and worms."

Penny gagged, spilling some juice from her mouth.

Headmaster Kepler took a mic at the end of the room and tapped on it gently. "Students! Welcome back to the school you never left in the first place. The irony isn't lost on any of us, but do understand that we all feel the strain of leaving our families behind for an entire school year. Only five more months until summer."

"Do you ever feel like we're prisoners here?" Penny leaned in and asked me. I don't think she was joking.

"We're going to have a fantastic second semester," Kepler continued. "As many of you have already noticed, the bug that started at the beginning of the year lingers even today. It's nothing to be concerned about. Our nurse has told me it's just a case of mild influenza that keeps cycling through everyone. It's strange, yes, but *not* harmful—you'll feel sweaty and tired is all. The nurse is still researching a cure, but in the meantime, let's not share any food or drinks. Wash your hands thoroughly, and practice good hygiene as best as you can."

I looked up from my tray, shocked that I hadn't noticed it earlier. I knew a few kids were sick, but it turned out that *a lot* of students had been infected.

"Man," I said. "That bug is really workin' overtime."

"You're right. Weird," Noah said. "When did that happen?"

"Apparently, it's been happening all year," I said. "How have we not really noticed this?"

Noah shrugged and went back to eating. "I just wasn't paying attention, I guess. I've been too busy working on creating fire without dried meat."

"Same here," Penny said. "Except replace his tire and dried meat with a mouse and my ukulele."

I looked at Jordan.

"I just don't care," he said.

I watched the sick kids shuffle across the banquet hall like they were cheap toys whose batteries were dying.

Something was off. Terribly, terribly off.

"There's kind of a mystery here, isn't there?" I said. "Maybe it's just the flu, but . . . what if it's not?"

Penny sighed. "Yeah, right, maybe you can solve the case of the sick Kepler kids. Your selfless act will probably make everyone forget about Barf-gate."

"You're right!" I said.

"What? No," Penny sighed. "I was *mocking* you, dude."

"Still! What if this is some kind of supervillain bug? I can totally save the day and be the hero! Kids won't call me 'Den Darfer' anymore!"

"A supervillain bug?" Penny repeated.

A glimmer of hope probably twinkled in my eye. I turned and nodded at a camera that wasn't there. "A supervillain bug."

CHAPTER THIRTY-SEVEN

A week later, I was in the game room watching Mae, the girl who could travel through glass. She looked tired, and her skin was pale and clammy. She had all the right symptoms.

My plan was to collect a sample of her clammy sweat and then, like, examine it or something. The second part of my plan was still a little fuzzy.

Mae sat on a bench by herself.

I snuck up behind her, trying to keep a low profile.

I acted like I was interested in something under the bench. She saw me but didn't think anything of it.

When she looked away, I took a wooden stick out of my back pocket and bent over to tie my shoe.

My shoe that *wasn't* untied.

Boom. Faked it.

Ever so gently, I scraped the stick up the back of her arm, collecting some clammy sweat.

I was holding a clue in my hand. The first clue in what I hoped to be a major case!

I stealthily brought the damp end of the Popsicle stick up to my nose and sniffed deeply to check if it smelled like worms.

Nope. Just strawberries.

And right then I realized Mae was gawking at me.

She did *not* look happy.

"O-M-Goodness, Ben, you *freak*," she cried.

I wanted to run, but my legs didn't get the message.

"I swear this isn't what it looks like. . . ." I said, smiling nervously.

"It looks like you're smelling my sweat on that stick!"

"Yes!" I said, and then immediately continued, "I mean, no! Sorry, darn autocorrect . . ."

Autocorrect? Why'd I say that? I wasn't even texting!

Mae tightened her mouth and balled her fists super tight.

"I'm sorry! I'm *so* sorry!" I said, flinching before Mae even did anything.

Thirty minutes later . . .

"And she just punched you in the face in front of everybody?" Noah asked.

"Yeaaaah . . ." I said. "But to be fair, I think I deserved it. Collecting a sweat sample for analysis was a bad idea."

"What'd it smell like?" Totes the Goat asked.

We were all in my dorm. Penny and Noah were planted on the couch playing Minecraft. Totes stood next to them, looking at me with his freakin' weird sideways pupils. I was crashed on my bed with an ice pack on my second black eye of the year, and Jordan was nowhere to be seen.

I looked at the goat. "Strawberries. But why are you even in here?"

"What? Just cuz I'm a goat, I can't hang with you guys? Ohhhh, the stupid goat just wants to eat stupid grass all day! Watch him scream like a human! . . . So offensive."

"Scream like a human?" I asked.

Penny hit Pause and spun around on the couch. "Dude, YouTube 'goats yelling like humans,' and thank me later."

"Give Totes a break," Noah said. "He misses Mine-craft, he's got no friends, and the upperclassmen always mess with him."

The goat's head snapped toward Noah. *"Thank you very much for telling everyone my business!"* he said *super* sarcastically.

"Yeah, Noah does that," I said.

Totes lowered his head and spoke quieter. "I miss Minecraft, plus . . . the upperclassmen *do* pick on me. They keep trying to ride me."

Oh, man! I never even *thought* about that, but I couldn't really ask Totes for a ride *right after* he said he hated it.

Maybe later.

"My investigation led me nowhere," I said.

"It led you to an important lesson about personal space," Penny joked.

"That's *all* it did!" I huffed. "I've been watchin' sick kids all week, but there's nothing really different about them. They have perfect attendance, and their grades are even better than mine!"

"That's not too hard, though," Noah said.

"Burn!" Penny said, and gave Noah the highest of fives.

"The sickos don't cause any trouble," I said. "They're not puking or anything. They're just . . . clammy, pale, and sleepy-looking."

Totes looked at me. "I've seen the kids you're talkin' about."

"Because there's, like, a billion of them?" I said.

The goat nodded.

I threw myself back on my bed and rubbed my face. "Ughhh, maybe I need a sidekick. The best detectives have them. Holmes and Watson. Batman and Robin. Ketchup and Mustard . . . if they were detectives."

"Ooooo! Mac and cheese!" Penny said.

"Hugs and kisses!" Noah chimed in.

"Chips and salsa!" Penny exclaimed. "I like this game!"

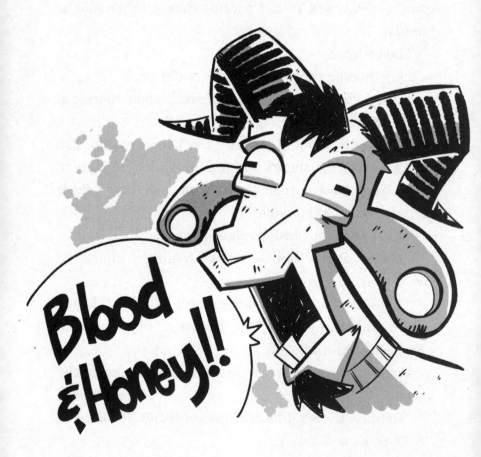

Blood & Honey!!

We all looked at the goat.

"No?" Totes said, bobbing his head, embarrassed. "Okay then . . . *not* blood and honey."

Jordan's voice suddenly cut through the room. "Wait, have you been investigating for the past week? Is that why you're never around? And why you've racked up a short stack of tardy slips?"

Penny jumped up from the couch and shouted while pointing her finger at different parts of the room. "Jordan! We told you if you wanna hang out with us, you can't be naked!"

"Oh, for—seriously?" Noah shouted without taking his eyes off the TV screen. "C'mon, man! Where are you?"

"Lying on my belly . . ." Jordan answered with a small voice. "On your bed."

Noah jumped up and pitched his controller across the room. "Get your naked butt off my stuff!"

The controller bounced off Jordan's invisible body as he laughed.

The front door opened, and Jordan ran into the hallway. Penny and Noah ran after him with a set of clothes, leaving me and Totes alone in the room.

I made a note to grab a pair of Professor Duncan's thermal goggles. He probably wouldn't even notice they were gone. I'd be able to see Jordan anywhere with them. He was invisible, but he couldn't hide the heat from his body.

But before then . . . I needed a sidekick, and there just happened to be one sitting in the room with me at that moment.

"Hey, goat," I said.

"Call me Totes, please."

"Totes. Wanna be my sidekick?"

The goat paused. ". . . go on."

"Um, that's it. You probably see students outside all the time. If you see something weird, come find me."

The goat paused again. ". . . go on."

"That's it!"

Totes bobbed his head up and down. "You got it."

The first warm day in March.

Noah, Penny, and I were on the roof of the school testing the metal discs Professor Duncan had created. An entire box full of different colored discs, and *none* of them had labels.

All we knew was that the pink ones exploded.

I won't say how. Just that it was awesome.

"Who invents things without keeping track of what they are?" I asked, pushing my hand through the discs.

"Someone who doesn't die," Penny answered, sitting on the edge of the roof, dangling her feet over the side.

"Pen, could you *not* hang over the edge of a ten-story building, please?" Noah said. "That's so unwizard of you! It's making my butt clench!"

"Does this scare you?" Penny asked, leaning over even more. "Stop saying 'wizard' and I'll back off the edge!"

Noah covered his face with his hands. "Okay, fine! I'll stop!"

She laughed and then looked down at the courtyard. "The school grounds look so dumpy from up here. You can really tell all the plants are dying when you're this high up. Abigail needs to step up her flower-kissing game."

"The front of the school is the same," I said, digging my hand into the box again. I grabbed a blue disc from the middle. "Who wants to test it?"

"Uh . . . *you* test it," Penny said. "Wasn't that the whole point? So *you* could fake powers? We *have* powers."

"Fine," I said, walking back to the shack. "There's a spider over here. I'll test it on him."

"This probably isn't smart," Noah said.

"No, you mean this probably isn't *safe*," I said, holding the disc over the M&M-size spider minding its own business in its web. It was tiny, but I was still freaked out by it. I *really* hate spiders. "Ready?"

Noah nodded. Penny did, too, but not until she was behind Noah.

I dropped the disc on top of the spider.

With a tiny puff of smoke, the spider disappeared. It reappeared a few feet behind me in the same puff of smoke.

"Sweet!" I said. "So the blue ones teleport."

I grabbed another disc from Duncan's box. A red one. Then I threw it at the spider. The disc sizzled when it made contact. With a loud *BOOM!*, the spider instantly became the size of a car.

And not a small one, but one of those giant boats old people drive.

"*Cheesy rice, that disc was like a Mario mushroom!*" Noah shouted.

The spider lurched up on its back legs and hissed at the three of us. It slammed back into the roof and crawled toward me, unfolding its gigantic fangs.

"I think you made it angry!" Noah shouted.

"Probably because you're throwing discs at it!" Penny bellowed. "I wish you knew some kind of martial art to fight the giant spider with! Some form of kung fu or something!"

Even under pressure, Penny had a smart mouth.

The spider lunged at me, trying to catch me with its

fangs, but I fell backward, dodging the attack. My fear
of spiders was cranked to eleven.

"Penny! Use your animal-control power to stop it!" I
yelled, rolling away from the spider.

"I control animals! Not insects!" Penny shouted as
the spider made its way toward her.

"Technically insects are animals!" Noah said.

"Technically I don't care!" Penny said. "I don't have
my uke anyway!"

With its two front legs, the spider grabbed Penny. As
it lifted her into the air, I could see the red disc stuck to
its back.

Penny was in trouble. It was time to face my fear.

"It's gonna eat me!!!" Penny screeched.

"Noah!" I said, running full speed toward the monster of my own accidental creation.

"On it!" Noah said, facing the spider. He punched his chest and let out a wretched burp, shooting a fireball over the spider's head.

It was just the distraction I needed to climb up the spider's body. I clutched its hairy shell as it spun around with Penny still in its clutches. The edge of the Lodge was dangerously close.

"Hang on, Pen!" I called out, reaching for the red disc. It was so close!

"*I hate you!*" Penny screamed.

My foot caught one of the spider's hind legs, and I launched myself farther up its body, just far enough to reach the red disc. My fingers scraped along the gross back of the spider, and the disc popped off.

Just like that, it was over.

The spider instantly shrunk back to the size of an M&M. Penny and I fell flat on our butts, only a few feet from the edge.

I clutched the red disc in my fist and raised it in the air. "Don't everybody thank me at once."

"Thank you?" Penny growled. "The whole thing was *your fault!*"

I pretended not to hear her and then thanked myself. "*Nice one*, Ben. *Thank you*, Ben. *You're welcome*, Ben. *Stop talking to yourself*, Ben."

Suddenly there was a *CRUNCH!* followed by a *ZIP!*

Professor Duncan had landed on his feet right next to us. He punched his arms out. Two metal cables retracted into leather bands around his forearms, making the same *ZIP!* sound as before.

"Whoa . . . those are like grappling hooks," I said.

"You guys okay?" Duncan asked, searching the rooftop. "I thought I saw a giant spider."

I laughed nervously, pushing the red disc into my

back pocket. "Hehe, uh, nope. No spiders or monsters or spider-monsters up here, thanks for asking."

Duncan eyeballed me.

I pointed to his armbands. "Can I try those?"

"Absolutely not," Duncan said as he walked back to the edge of the roof. "Oh, and kids? I seem to be missing a pair of thermal goggles. I'm not saying anyone on the *roof* has them . . . just that I'm missing them. And I hope they turn up soon."

He knew about the goggles.

Whoopsies.

Duncan held his foot off the edge and let himself drop.

Noah, Penny, and I ran to the side just in time to see Duncan stretch his arms out. Two metal wires shot out of the armbands, anchoring into the side of the Lodge. His body swung down and slowed almost to a stop a few feet off the grass in the courtyard.

With another snap of his wrists, the metal wires retracted, and he landed safely on the ground.

Duncan walked away like the cool guy does when he knows everybody's watching.

Dang it.

I wish I were that cool.

CHAPTER THIRTY-NINE

Someone knocked at my door.

At first, I thought maybe Noah got locked out after getting a midnight snack or something, but he was fast asleep in his bunk.

I stared at the line of light under my door. A shadow moved outside it.

I dropped to the floor and tiptoed past the couch where Jordan slept. He had been bunking with us because he didn't want to stay in his room with Dexter. A blanket draped over nothingness, and his pillow was pushed in under his head. A small dark spot showed on the fabric where he drooled.

Could it be Penny? No. She usually sent mice through the hole in her floor to wake us by nibbling on our ears.

She thought it was hilarious to do that at three in the morning.

It's not.

I peeked through the peephole, surprised to see the knocker. It was weird enough that I rubbed my eyes and checked again.

I opened the door.

Totes the Goat sat on his butt, smiling at me. "Hey, sidekick, remember when you—"

"Wait, you're *my* sidekick. I'm not yours."

"What? When did *that* happen?"

"At the very beginning. When I asked *you* to be *mine*."

"So if I'm *your* sidekick, what does that make you?"

"Your boss," I said with a smile.

"Mmmm, no," the goat said, shaking his head. "I

don't like that. Let's just say we're *sidekicks*. Like, I'm yours and you're mine."

I heard Jordan snort from the couch. I didn't wanna wake him up, so I nodded at Totes.

"Fine," I said. "What do you want?"

I stepped into the hallway and held the door open with my foot.

Totes explained everything.

"I was outside trying to sleep, right?" Totes said.

"When I saw a kid walk into the forest behind the school, right? It's *way* past curfew, so I knew something weird was going on, right? The kind of 'weird' that you asked me to keep an eye out for, right?"

"Right." I patted Totes on the head. "Gooooood, goat! You did good! Meet me in the courtyard in five minutes."

"Roger, roger."

I snuck back into my dorm to grab Duncan's thermal goggles, which I hadn't returned yet.

Whoopsies . . . again.

I slipped them over my eyes and flipped the switch on the side.

There was a flash of green as the goggles warmed up. Within seconds, I could see everything in the room. It was all cast in a green tint, which made heat signatures easily visible. I saw Noah's body colored in reds and yellows as he slept in his bed. Jordan's was the same on the couch.

After that, I headed out to meet Totes in the courtyard.

Ten minutes later, Totes and I were standing at the edge of the forest behind the school. It was so quiet you could hear an eyeball blink.

"He went out there?" I said, still wearing my jammies along with a pair of flip-flops.

"That he did," the goat said, turning around and walking back toward the school.

"Wait, you're not coming?"

"Are you kidding?" Totes said without breaking his stride. "Forests scare the pee outta me."

I faced the dark trees of the forest, slipping the thermal goggles back over my eyes.

I was alone, cold, and frightened.

But I looked crazy cool with my goggles.

CHAPTER FORTY

A.fter only a few minutes in the forest, I heard the footsteps of the mystery kid.

Dropping to my knees in the brush, I scanned the area for any flashes of red or yellow in the thermal vision.

Nothing.

Just a couple of squirrels, an owl, and, like, a zillion white golf balls.

I crawled along the ground like a shivering ninja over dried leaves and twigs until I bumped into a short stone wall overgrown with vines.

It looked like a campfire pit.

In the middle of the forest.

Someone didn't think that through.

My vision was all green. No heat signatures anywhere nearby.

"Dang it," I said, disappointed that I lost the kid.

But when I pulled the goggles up on my forehead, I saw him right on the other side of the fire pit.

Dexter Dunn.

He was drenched in shadow, kneeling on the ground with his bare toes curled and buried in the dirt, and he was . . . chewing on a handful of earthworms?

What?! Who does that?

I stared at Dexter, doing my best to stay still even when my brain was screaming at me to run away.

Dexter didn't move. He just slurped away on those slippery, squishy, disgusting, super nasty earthworms. It was worse when I heard him swallow.

Ahhhhhg, so freakin' gross!

I forced my trembling fingers to pull the thermal goggles back over my eyes and flipped the switch.

I missed Dexter earlier because I was looking for red and yellow. Now that I knew what I was looking at, his dark green outline was right there in the visor.

I knew the goggles weren't broken, because the earthworms he chomped on were colored correctly.

That kid had no heat signature.

You know what else has no heat signature?

Dead people.

Okay, but obviously Dexter wasn't dead, right? He was eating worms in the middle of the forest. With dead people, the opposite happens.

I adjusted the goggles and looked again. That was when I realized he wasn't the only person in the forest.

There were dozens of them. Other kids I recognized. Rose. Toby. Arnold. Even the nurse and Vice Principal Archer. They were all barefoot with their toes curled and planted in the dirt.

None of them had heat signatures.

The stones under my fingers crumbled and sent pebbles rolling.

All the shadowed figures snapped their heads in my direction.

"This is how I die?" I whispered.

The fire pit split open with a low rumble, pouring blue light across the forest. Obviously, some kind of secret entrance, but to what?

The worm-eaters scattered, disappearing deeper into the forest. I ran, too, or at least I *tried* to run. Flip-flops were a bad idea.

I ducked behind the nearest tree, hoping to hide from whatever was about to come out of that pit.

A hunched shadow of a man pulled itself up and dusted itself off. The man sighed deeply as the pit slid shut behind him, making the forest dark again.

The wind picked up. The leaves rustled.

He turned his head in my direction.

For what felt like forever, he stood there staring at nothing.

Any sudden movements from me and I'd stick out worse than Darth Vader at Luke's tenth birthday party.

I held perfectly still. My lungs started to ache from holding my breath.

Then he ruffled his coat and walked briskly back toward the school.

I exhaled slowly and peeked out from the tree. Through the goggles, I could see his face clearly—red-and-yellow heat signature and everything.

It was Donald Kepler.

CHAPTER FORTY-ONE

I was still in the courtyard, jammies on my body, flip-flops on my feet, and thermal goggles on my forehead.

I had hid in the bushes all night, waiting to see if those kids without heat signatures would show up again. They did not.

I saw Noah and Penny walking, so I hissed at them from the bushes.

"Psst!"

Penny stopped and looked around like she wasn't sure if she was hearing things.

"Pssssssst!"

"Ben?" Penny said, walking toward the bush. "Is that you?"

"Yes! Come here!"

"Dude, what the heck?" Noah said. "You weren't in bed when I woke up this morning. Have you been out here all night?"

I nodded.

"*Why?*"

"There's something *huge* happening here, guys," I whispered.

"Why are you whispering?" Penny said.

"Because! *He* could be listening!"

Penny paused. "Who's *he*?"

"Headmaster Kepler," I said. "I saw him last night! He walked out of his secret lair and—"

"Whoa, what?" Noah said. "He has a secret lair?"

"Yes! I was in the woods last night, and—"

"You were in the woods after dark?" Noah said.

"Yes, because I was following a kid who—"

"There was someone else out here, too?"

"Yes!" I shouted. I took a deep breath and unloaded everything on my friends at superspeed.

When I finished, Noah and Penny just stared.

"What?" Penny said, confused.

"Worm-eaters?" Noah said. "Kepler coming out of a secret lair in the forest? Did you sleep at all last night?"

I shook my bloodshot eyes and rubbed my head. "No."

"I thought you fixed that by crying yourself to sleep," Penny said.

My wide eyes darted at Noah. "Dude!"

Penny shrugged. "He didn't tell me. I can hear you through the hole in my floor."

Noah nodded and pointed to Penny.

"Whatever!" I said. "Something *bad* is happening here!"

Noah looked at the other students in the courtyard. "If something bad was happening, I think we'd be able to see it."

"That's just it," I said, tripping out of the bush. "Nobody's looking for it! Everyone's too busy with themselves and their own powers to notice the kids who *aren't* using their powers!"

Penny and Noah shared a glance. It was subtle, but it was there.

"This is a big deal!" I said. "Why aren't you guys saying anything?"

"Because you sound bonkersville," Penny said.

Just then, some random boy walked up and joined us. He gave me a half smile, which I politely returned. He was a bit taller than me, with a thin face and messy blond hair.

Noah smiled back. Penny waved. It was a little weird that someone new decided to stand with us, but whatever.

We were quiet, looking back and forth at each other, unsure about the new kid.

"Who're you?" I asked, trying to be polite.

"Jordan," he answered.

"Whoa!" I said. "You figured out how to control your power! We can totally see your face!"

"Yeah," Penny said. "You're not as ugly as I thought you'd be. Congrats."

But Jordan didn't show the excitement I thought he would. "Yeah. Sure. Whatever."

His face was hard to read, but then again, it was the first time I had ever seen it.

He had blue eyes and pale skin. Like, sick pale. And

he looked sweaty. No . . . he looked clammy. And there was a hint of worms in the air.

My stomach sunk. Slowly, I brought my hands up and stretched them over my head. "Hey, what's that?" I said, pointing across the courtyard.

My friends all looked away at the same time. While they were distracted, I pulled the thermal goggles over my eyes.

Penny and Noah's heat signatures were normal, with shades of red and yellow.

But Jordan was different. . . .

Jordan had no heat signature at all.

I laughed nervously as I took off the thermal goggles and let them hang from my neck. "Ha, ha! You guys are so funny with your *heat* signatures. . . . Warm bodies! Warm bodies all around!"

Noah cocked an eye. "You need some sleep."

I grabbed Noah's and Penny's shirtsleeves and pulled them away from Jordan. "Welp, we gotta get to class. See ya, dude!"

Jordan didn't care, or if he did, I couldn't tell. He just blinked at us as we walked off.

"Hey," Penny said, pulling her arm free. "You're hurting me!"

"What're you doing?" Noah said. "Why can't Jordan come with us?"

"Remember when I said I saw those kids without heat signatures?" I asked.

"Uh, yup," Penny said. "You only told us, like, twenty seconds ago."

"Right!" I said. "Jordan's been staying in our dorm

all year. I've *seen* his heat signature before with these goggles."

"So?" Noah asked.

"So Jordan *didn't* have one just now!" I explained. "He was like the rest of those worm-eaters! Walking dead bodies!"

Noah shook his head. "He's *not* dead. He was just talking to us. If he was a zombie, he'd look like this. . . ."

"I don't know what's going on with Jordan and the rest of the sick kids," I said, "but I know that Kepler's behind it. He's *gotta* be! He was in the woods last night when I saw the rest of those creepy cold kids!"

"Gimme those things, Braver," Penny said, grabbing

the goggles that were strung around my neck. She pressed them against her eyes and looked back at Jordan.

"Kepler . . . is an *evil supervillain*," I said confidently.

"Do you have to say '*evil*' before '*supervillain*'?" Penny asked. "Isn't '*supervillain*' enough?"

"Fine," I said. "Kepler . . . is a *supervillain* . . . And he's *evil*."

CHAPTER FORTY-TWO

I was on my own in front of Kepler Academy, hangin' out with Brock. It was the first time all year. The last time I visited, he was covered in snow.

"Sorry I've been avoiding you," I said.

Brock didn't mind.

"But some stuff has come up. Some *big* stuff. Like, possibly *shutting down the academy* big stuff. Jordan's in danger, and I think Kepler's behind it, but I have no proof."

Same ol' Brock, bein' all quiet.

"You're right. I need to *get* proof, but how? I guess I could find a way into his secret hideout. I mean, I can't do *nothing*, right?"

Brock's silence was killing me . . . softly.

"If it'll help Jordan and the rest of the infected kids, then breaking into Kepler's secret base is the *right* thing to do, but . . . I could get into a ton of trouble, and not the kind where I clean the school yard for a day. The kind where my parents have to identify the body.

"And what if busting Kepler starts a chain reaction

where he becomes the most powerful supervillain in the world. What if he goes nuts and destroys the planet?"

Brock. Nothing.

"So . . . should I do it?" I asked.

And then the craziest thing happened—a tiny pebble fell from his stone face.

I took it as a sign. I knew, without a doubt, what I had to do.

"You're right. I owe it to Jordan. He'd do it for me. I'm gonna break into Kepler's hideout."

I sat in front of the statue, studying Brock's stone face.

"Thanks for listening."

CHAPTER FORTY-THREE

1 a.m.

Go Time.

Noah, Penny, and I snuck through the courtyard in the dead of night. After my talk with Brock, I came up with a plan and filled them in.

Noah nibbled on a beef jerky stick in case we needed him to breathe fire.

Penny had her uke in case we were . . . attacked by mice?

And I had a bag of gadgets I "borrowed" from Professor Duncan. I was also wearing my Halloween costume because I looked super heroic.

At the edge of the courtyard, I turned to look at the school. If everything went according to plan, I wasn't sure what was going to happen to the academy. If Kepler was the bad guy, then the school was gonna change.

I didn't know if that was a good thing or a bad thing, but I knew I needed to take one last look at it. If things *didn't* go as planned, then it was probably the last time I'd see it.

A minute later, we were at the fire pit in the forest.

"So how do we get in?" Penny asked.

"I don't know," I whispered, running my fingers along the stones of the fire pit. "It slides open, but there's no switch or anything. Maybe it's voice-activated? No, that's too spy movie. This is evil supervillain stuff we're talkin' about."

"Just supervillain," Penny corrected.

"Can you get some mice to open it from the inside?" I asked.

Penny shook her head. "They'll do what I tell them to do, but I don't know what the inside of this thing looks like, so I can't really tell them to flip a latch or something."

"It's cool," I said, shaking my bag upside down and letting everything fall out.

I sifted through Duncan's gadgets, looking for something that could be useful. I knew through the process of agonizingly painful elimination exactly what each color did.

For the task at hand, I thought a yellow disc would do the trick.

"The yellow ones make a bubble shield," I said. "Stand back. When I turn this on, it'll make an energy bubble that'll cut through anything it touches."

"You're gonna carve out an entrance," Noah said, nodding. "Nice."

I didn't wanna gloat, but I did for a second. "I'm pretty smart."

Noah and Penny stood at a safe distance.

I stood at the center of the fire pit.

"Three—two—one," I said, then I pinched the disc firmly.

The shield opened, creating a perfect bubble around me, cutting through the fire pit under my feet.

With another pinch, the bubble shield deactivated, and the broken-up stones crumbled away, dropping me like a bad habit.

I reached out and caught myself before falling into the tunnel. Penny helped me back out.

We all peered into the dark abyss of Kepler's secret

hideout. Metal rungs were built into the wall leading the way down.

"You ready?" I asked my friends.

They both nodded, but I could see fear in their eyes. They could probably see it in mine, too.

"What if he's down there?" Noah asked.

"The lights are out," I said. "The last time I saw Kepler come outta here, the lights were so bright they burned my eyes."

Penny looked at me. "We can still go back to the school. We don't have to do this. We can find Abigail. She's head of security anyway."

"No," I said. "Abigail's been infected, too. She's sick and smells like worms like the rest of them."

I thought about Jordan and the other students at Kepler Academy. What if this wasn't the first year Kepler had done this? What if students in the past had been infected with whatever it was this year's students were infected with? Abigail *did* say the bug swept through the school every year. There was *so much* at stake.

"No," I continued. "I'm going down. You guys can turn back if you want. I won't tell anyone you were even with me."

Penny made a face. "Like we're gonna let you go down there alone." She pointed in the direction of the school. "It's their time—*their time* up here, but it's our time—*our time* down there."

I gasped at Penny's *Goonies* reference, which *might* or *might not* have made me pee a little. Eighties treasure-hunting movies are the best.

I slid my feet over the edge and found a metal rung.

My act 3 was at the bottom of that tunnel, and I didn't want to keep it waiting.

CHAPTER FORTY-FOUR

The climb down was far.

After a bunch of metals rungs, my foot touched a concrete floor. I pushed aside the crumbled stone and helped Penny and Noah down.

"It's pitch black in here," Penny said. She grabbed my hand and held it.

Can't say I didn't like it.

"I brought flashlights in my—" I said, stopping when I realized my goodie bag was back at the top of the ladder. "I forgot all my stuff up there!"

"Just find the light switch," Penny said.

"No!" I said, squeezing Penny's hand tightly. To my surprise, she squeezed back. "Someone might see the light if we turn it on!"

"So what do we do?" Penny asked.

"Hang on," Noah called from the dark. He was across the room somewhere. "Just gimme one . . . second . . ."

A burst of fire erupted about ten feet away. My eyes adjusted, and I saw Noah cradling a fireball above his hand.

"*When did you learn to do that?!*" I said, jealous.

Noah acted like it was nothing. "Couple of weeks ago. I've been keeping it up my sleeve for the right time to show it off."

The fireball cast a yellow glow across the room.

We were definitely standing in Kepler's secret lair. The younger pictures of him gave it away.

Buzzing machines and secret laboratory concoctions oozing out of beakers are what I *expected* to see, but it wasn't that at all. The Kepler Cave was just a plain old filthy room with cobwebs and dust everywhere.

The only furniture was a desk that had been over-turned, the wood splintered. Broken glass covered the floor.

Newspaper clippings and framed photos hung on the walls.

Penny pulled out her cell phone and started snapping pictures. "Hashtag, evidence," she said.

I looked through the photos of Kepler and his friends. They were old, from back when the academy first opened. The Lodge hadn't changed much since then.

The biggest photo was of Kepler standing behind the first fourteen students of the academy. The smaller pictures were of the children practicing their powers as Kepler watched.

"Wait," I said, recounting the kids in the main photo. "The first class had fourteen kids, right?"

"Yeah," Noah said, squinting at another article.

"There's fifteen kids in this photo with Kepler," I said. "Who's the extra kid?"

Noah studied the photo with me. "Huh . . . weird . . . maybe he accidentally enrolled?"

"Like me?" I said. "Someone with no powers?"

"Maybe," Noah said. "Must not have lasted long since he's not part of the history of the school."

Noah's words stung. I'd hate to end up like the fifteenth kid—unremarkable and forgotten.

The framed photos ended on one wall, and we moved

to the next one, which was filled with laminated news-paper articles. I wasn't sure what exactly I was looking at.

They were definitely newspaper articles, but with stories of things that never happened. Stories with pictures of costumed superheroes posing after saving the day. There were even articles about the death and destruction of major cities in the world.

"These are all fake articles," I said. "Look at this one. . . . NEW YORK CITY RAVAGED BY THE SCREAM QUEEN."

Penny snapped another picture. "Here's one that says San Francisco was swallowed up by the ocean."

The rest of the articles were just as fake. Kennedy saved from assassination. The first man on the moon wasn't Neil Armstrong, but some superhero who literally flew there instead. The Vietnam War ended by the involvement of superheroes.

"They're old newspaper clippings," Noah said. "And look at this one here. . . . Is that Abigail?"

The person in the fake article *was* Abigail. A much younger version, but definitely her. A skintight costume clung to her body. Nine other people wearing similar costumes were with her, posing in front of a monument dedicated to the lives lost in the Battle of San Francisco.

"What are we looking at?" Noah said, dumbfounded. "*None* of these things happened. New York and LA haven't been destroyed."

"He's crazy," I said, feeling my brain wrinkle. "Kepler created this school to teach people how to hide their powers, but what if it's all a scam? What if he's doing it just so he can be the most powerful superhero?"

"Ben," Penny said, pointing at another laminated article. "He doesn't want to be a super*hero*. . . . He wants to be a super*villain*."

Kepler's young face frowned from the center of the article. He looked roughed up, with a deep gash cut across the bridge of his nose. He was holding a sign with his name and random numbers across the bottom.

It was a police mug shot.

The smaller photos underneath showed Kepler behind bars.

The fake articles after that took a dark turn. More major cities in the world destroyed. Superheroes falling at the hands of a villain called the Reaper.

The last newspaper page was the most messed up.

There weren't any articles after that.

We were speechless. Kepler had created this whole story where everyone in the world died.

He was the headmaster of the academy.

Our leader.

And he was insane.

CHAPTER FORTY-FIVE

My knees felt weak as I stared at the fake newspaper articles.

I took off my cape and mask and let them fall to the ground. I didn't feel like playing superhero anymore.

Kepler was nuts, and I trusted him. We all did.

And everyone was still in trouble, sick with the Kepler bug. After seeing the shrine he built to himself, I was sure he was the one behind it all.

The edge of my cape fluttered slightly, like it was calling out to me from the floor.

Noah read the articles aloud as Penny snapped pictures at warp speed.

"'Witnesses say an unknown super appeared in the Chicago skyline late Thursday night, where he floated for seven days,'" Noah said. "'His dark cloak and hood, which covered his face, earned him the name the Reaper. Attempts to contact the super failed. Even attempts by other supers.'"

"He just floated there?" Penny asked.

I knelt down next to my quivering cape. That's when

I felt a weak draft along the floor. I slid my fingers across the smooth concrete to find where it was coming from.

"Yeah," Noah said. "It says he didn't even move. He was like some kind of floating statue. But then things took a violent turn when the Comet Kid got fed up and tried to attack the mystery dude."

"Comet Kid?" Penny asked. "That's a lame name even for a *fake* story. What happened after that?"

"The Reaper vaporized Comet Kid," Noah said. "And then he leveled all of Chicago. Turned it into a barren wasteland."

At the edge of the room, I pressed my face against the floor. The cold draft teased my cheek. That air was coming from somewhere.

I scratched at a spot on the ground where the wall met the floor, tearing out chunks of concrete. I could feel air blowing harder through the small cracks.

The smell of worms was thick.

"Wait, where's Ben?" Penny asked from across the room.

"I'm right over—" I started to say but got cut off. I had just opened up a sinkhole.

Everything went black as I fell through the floor. I tried to reach for anything to grab onto, but my arms were pinned against my body by the wet dirt and rocks.

Lucky for me, the trip wasn't long. Ten—maybe twelve—feet later, I felt the sinkhole open up, and I face-planted into the cold dirt.

I was in a small cave that had tunnels running down several different sides. From one of the tunnels, a soft red light pulsed, painting the rock walls in a horror-movie-blood-red color.

"Ben!" Noah shouted down the shaft from Kepler's lair. "Are you okay?"

I got up on my knees.

And then something caught my eye.

Something that shouldn't have been down there.

On the floor about fifteen feet in front of me was a single sneaker. Not old and gnarly, but clean and shiny. Fresh. Like it was bought yesterday.

A scene like that is how scary movies end. A circus clown with fangs will jump out of the shadows. The screen will go black. The credits will roll with no music.

I was dripping with fear. My heart pounded as I crawled to the shoe. The throbbing red light reflected off the white vegan leather.

"But where's your twin?" I asked the shoe like it would answer.

The small cave opened up to an enormous cavern where the red light was coming from.

Dozens of red egg-shaped plants spread out across the floor, each about three feet tall. It was the light pulsing from inside the eggs that cast the red death-glow. The stank smell of worms made my head hurt.

As the light in the shells glowed brighter, I saw shapes inside. Big shapes. Human-size shapes. I pressed my face against one of the red eggs.

When the light pulsed, I saw Dexter Dunn inside, curled up like a baby. I didn't know whether he was dead or alive.

Horrified, I stumbled back into a different egg, where Rose was curled up. Another had Toby. Vic. Mae. Every red egg pulsed with a kid inside.

I felt sick. It was too much. I wanted to run. To forget everything I'd seen in the last ten minutes.

I was standing in the middle of a cemetery filled with students from Kepler Academy.

CHAPTER FORTY-SIX

I was still trying not to puke when Noah caught up to me.

"Dude, you're okay," he said, relieved. "Penny went to get help because we were afraid you died or something."

I shook my head and pointed at the eggs. "You're not far off."

Noah looked at the pods. His face said more than words could.

"What the what . . . what is all this?" he whispered.

"Students," I said.

"Are they dead?" he asked.

"Yes. I think so. I don't know."

Noah pressed his face against Dexter's egg. He stared into it for a moment. "His chest is moving up and down! He's breathing!"

Noah and I checked the other eggs. Everyone was still alive.

A tidal wave of relief washed over me.

"So Kepler's a villain. He's replaced most of the students with his worm-eaters," I said. "That's why they don't have heat signatures! That's why nobody has realized the kids have gone missing. The fake versions probably don't have powers, but nobody noticed because kids aren't allowed to use powers anyway."

"But what's he want with these kids?" Noah asked.

"Sustenance . . ."

Noah looked at me. "I can't tell if you're joking or not."

I wasn't.

Penny called from the side of the cavern. "Ben! You're okay!"

I smiled until I saw who she'd brought back with her.

Abigail.

The head of security was tired and grumpy, with purple bags under her eyes and clammy skin like the other worm-eaters.

"How'd you get down here?" Noah asked.

Penny threw her thumb over her shoulder. "There's a staircase back there. Abigail knew about it. She was patrolling the school grounds when I went to get help."

I stared at Abigail. If she was infected, then she'd show other signs, too. Shuffling her feet like a dying toy or mumbling one-word answers.

"Stop gawking at me like that, Ben," she said.

"Oh, good," I said, letting out a breath of air. "You're not infected. You're just frumpy."

"Excuse me?"

"Nothing!" I said.

"You children *shouldn't* be down here," she said, examining the cavern walls. "These caves are abandoned gold mines. No one has been down here for a hundred years."

"That's not true," I said. "Kepler's been laying eggs down here."

Penny made a face. "Whoa, hold up. I told Abigail about his hideout, but now he's laying eggs? What did I miss?"

"Yes, Ben, what are you talking about?" Abigail asked, concerned.

"I'm talking about Kepler kidnapping students," I said. "I don't know how or why, but he's replacing them with worm-eaters!"

"Worm-eaters? Kidnapping?" Abigail repeated. "Do you know how ridiculous you sound?"

"Look in the eggs yourself," Noah said.

Abigail walked through the pods, running her fingers over the tops of them. Kneeling next to Dexter's pod, she gazed inside. "I stand corrected," she said quietly.

"That's why we need to stop him!" I said.

Abigail tightened her lips. "You're right. Donald *must* be stopped, but . . . do you have a plan for that?"

"Uh, that's why you're here," I said.

"Of course, but we need proof that this is all *his* doing."

"This whole cave is *full* of proof."

"This is all circumstantial. This cave of eggs under his hideout might just be a coincidence. You need solid evidence because that man is a good liar."

"Then we'll call him out in front of the whole school. Villains always confess under that kind of pressure."

"This isn't a comic book, Ben," Abigail said. "This is real life. Cornering someone like that could make them snap."

"But we need to catch him off-guard! If he knows we're coming, he'll run," I said, making my way to the stairs.

Noah followed.

"Ben, wait!" Abigail shouted. *"Benjamin!"*

It was Penny's voice that stopped me in my tracks. *"Ben!"*

Noah and I looked back at the same time.

Without warning, Abigail slapped her hand over Penny's mouth and forced her to the ground.

The dirt under Penny cracked as thick green vines slithered out like giant snakes. They wrapped around her body as she struggled to break free.

"Ben! Help me!" she cried out.

"Penny!" I shouted, trying to run forward, but Noah held me back.

"No, don't!" he said.

The green vines that wrapped around Penny fused together, becoming red and transparent like the other eggs. I watched as Penny's body twitched inside until she stopped moving completely.

"I'm afraid I can't let you leave," Abigail said at the exact same time as someone else behind Noah and me.

A girl blocked our path to the stairs. Her skin was pale and clammy like a slug, and her eyes were glazed over and cloudy. She had Penny's face but spoke Abigail's words.

"How's that for a plot twist?" Abigail said through the smirking face of Evil Penny.

CHAPTER FORTY-SEVEN

Noah and I stood side by side, facing the head-of-security-turned-evil Abigail.

Evil Penny pushed us forward. "Welcome to my science experiment," she said in unison with Abigail.

Abigail was controlling the worm-eaters!

"Why are you doing this?" I said.

Abigail's forehead wrinkled. "Because I can? Because I've wasted my life doing things *his* way."

"Is Penny okay in there?"

"Oh, she's fine," Abigail said, running her fingers through her frizzy hair. "They're *all* fine. They wouldn't be much use to me if they *weren't*."

"Much use to you?" I said.

Evil Penny led us across the cavern to Abigail and her pods, like sheep to the slaughter.

"You're the first to witness my *rebirth*," Abigail said like a crazy person. "I *want* what Donald has taken from me. And now, under his own *lair*—under his own *nose*—I've collected an army to take back the life I could've had."

"You're taking these kids for your army?" Noah said.

"Do you hear yourself?" I asked. "You sound *ba-nay-nay!* You're like a comic book villain!"

Abigail's eye twitched. "How *dare* you speak to me like I'm some kind of *character* in a *story. Do you know what I'm capable of?*" She plucked a hair off the top of my head.

"All I need is the DNA from someone else to create their double," she said. "A single hair does the trick. It did for Penny when she found me earlier. She was so scared for you, Ben. Said I needed to come quick. That poor Benjamin Braver was hurt. . . . She was out of breath and nearly in tears. . . ."

Abigail knelt down, picked up a chunk of dirt, and

cupped it in her hand. Pressing her lips together, she spit into it. Then, with a motherly smile, she pushed my strand of hair into the wet spot.

Her face tightened. She raised the clod of dirt over her head and slapped it down as hard as she could, massaging it like dough until . . . it moved by itself.

She stepped back as the mud bubbled. It grew larger, taking the shape of a body. Arms and legs pulled away from the core, and a head emerged from the shoulders.

It took only seconds for the monster to be born.

Abigail's creation.

The worm-eater version of me.

CHAPTER FORTY-EIGHT

I was face-to-face with my evil twin, grown from a strand of hair and a loogie.

Evil Ben's toes were curled and half buried in the ground, just like the kids back in the forest.

WHOA...

They were plants! *That's* how they were grown. It was probably how they fed, too. That and also munching on worms.

"Destroy them," Abigail commanded Evil Penny and Evil Ben.

No time to hesitate.

I booted Evil Ben in the chest, sending him backward into Abigail.

Noah spun around and opened his mouth, burping a fireball that set Evil Penny on fire. She hissed as she fell to the ground, writhing around until she stopped moving.

My heart broke. Evil Penny was just a plant, but she still looked exactly like the real one.

Noah and I raced across the cavern to get to the staircase. We slid to a stop at the bottom step. The rest of Abigail's worm-eater army was blocking our path.

The two of us switched direction and bolted through the pods and past Abigail. The only other way out was the tunnel back to Kepler's secret room.

Abigail's words came from the mouths of all the worm-eaters in a creepy chorus. "You have such spirit, Ben! I envy that, I truly do, but this hope you have right now? It's worthless. You *hope* to escape. You *hope* to find Donald. You *hope* to see the sun rise again. . . . But *none* of those things will happen. How does it feel to know these are the last moments of your life?"

The nightmare fuel was strong with that woman.

We stopped at the sinkhole that led back to Kepler's room.

"Go!" I said, pushing Noah into the tunnel. "I'm right behind you!"

Noah clawed at the dirt and pulled his feet up, planting them against the walls.

The earth crumbled under his feet. I wasn't sure it was even solid enough for him to climb.

I grabbed his ankles and put my shoulders under his shoes. "Jump!"

Noah knelt down and jumped off my shoulders as high as he could, making it more than halfway up the tunnel.

Abigail's army was closing in.

There wasn't enough time for me to climb up, but only one of us needed to get away. Penny's life depended on it.

And, y'know, the other kids, too.

Noah reached his hand out to me from the top. "Hurry!"

I looked up at my best friend. He knew what I was thinking.

"Ben, don't!" he shouted.

But I was already kicking at the dirt walls.

Noah's muffled shouts faded away as the tunnel caved in.

I sprinted farther into the cavern, making as much noise as possible to hide Noah's shouting from the worm-eaters so they'd follow me instead of going after him.

They called to me as I ran. Their voices bounced off the walls, spanking my eardrums.

BEN BRAVER WHERE ARE YOUUUUUU...

Suddenly the floor disappeared from under my feet. I spun around, slamming down on my chest as I slid over the edge of a cliff I couldn't see, barely catching the ledge before going over.

I don't know how deep the drop was, but the rocks that fell past me never hit any floor I could hear.

The worm-eaters stopped at the edge, shuffling their feet as they searched for me.

At the top of the shaft, a giant hole opened up to the night sky. The full moon floated overhead, pouring soft light over the rock walls.

I hung there for minutes, my fingers burning with pain. The worm-eaters shuffled back and forth but weren't leaving. They knew I was there somewhere.

They were looking for me.

Their shuffling feet, smacking lips, and wheezing breath against the backdrop of silence was a nightmare.

And then suddenly, the school's alarm sounded in the distance. Noah had made it back safely. Kepler was on his way with his own secret army. Probably.

All I had to do was stay hidden, except my excitement gave me away.

I gasped when I heard the alarm.

A hand clutched my hair and pulled me up.

It was Evil Ben.

He dropped me on my butt as the army of worm-eaters formed a circle around me, faces lit by the moon.

I scooted backward, knocking a few of the plant people over the edge and into the abyss.

Abigail spoke through Evil Ben. "Are you done?"

I ignored her as I tugged on another worm-eater's jeans, yanking her back until she slipped off the cliff. She didn't even fight it.

"Do you think this is going to stop me?" Abigail said through another worm-eater.

And then another. "These are just plants! I can easily regrow them in no time!"

Every sentence came from a different worm-eater.

"I control my beautiful plants with my mind," Evil Vic said with a low chuckle.

Evil Dexter spoke. "It's a talent I didn't discover until the beginning of this year. Funny how old dogs *can* learn new tricks."

"What exactly *is* your trick?" I asked.

"I create life," Abigail said softly through my evil twin. "I could only ever *breathe* life into flowers. . . . But I've learned to *create* life now."

"They're my children, and I am their mother—their queen," Abigail's words came from Rose's lips. "But it's not easy to control *so* many of them at once. It's gotten harder as the year went on. . . ."

Abigail was monologuing. Classic villain move. It's when they just blah-blah-blah their whole plan, pretty much giving everything away. There's no risk in bragging to someone who was about to die anyway. . . .

Ah, dang it. . . .

Right then and there, I realized Abigail wasn't planning to let me leave. I had to keep her talking if I didn't want my story to end in an abandoned gold mine

"That's why the school yard looks like a plant cemetery," I said. "And why you've been such a hot mess."

Evil Rose slapped my face.

"You've got *such* a mouth on you," she sneered.

"And here we thought *Kepler* was the villain," I said.

The worm-eaters perked up at the same time, suddenly interested.

Evil Rose spoke. "Oh, he is. You have no idea, but I'm going to undo everything he's done using students from his own school. I'm going to wake up the world."

"Why don't you just build an army of your spit wad soldiers?"

"Because they're too frail. . . . They've served their purpose. I have the children I need now."

"Trapping these kids is one thing. Getting them on your side is something you probably don't have the power to do."

"You're right. *I* don't have the power to do that. . . . But there's *another* who does."

Of course Abigail wasn't the only villain. That would've made things too simple.

Evil Ben gripped his fingers around my neck and lifted me into the air, holding me over the bottomless cavern.

"I'm sorry, Ben. I wish you would've known me before this. I was a better person in another life. . . ."

"Wait! Please!" I whimpered as I tried prying Evil Ben's fingers off my neck. They were too strong. Like, *gorilla* strong.

How was it fair that the fake version of me had superstrength, but I didn't?

"Abigail, wait!" I said again, writhing around. "You don't have to do this!"

"I know I don't *have* to. . . ." Evil Ben said. And then he smirked. "But I *want* to."

My evil twin let go.

I reached out and grabbed his arm before I fell.

He took his other hand and tried prying me off, but I

was like a kid who didn't wanna go in the pool. I wrapped my legs around him and clung for dear life.

Evil Ben suddenly stopped struggling with me.

Abigail didn't care about the other worm-eaters falling to their deaths.

She didn't care about this one, either.

He smiled as he stepped off the edge of the cliff.

CHAPTER FORTY-NINE

My evil twin laughed hysterically as we fell down the dark shaft.

"I'm going to have front-row seats to this!" Abigail said through him. He wrapped his arms around me and held tighter.

I had no idea how deep the shaft was, but I knew I didn't wanna find out.

I shoved my hands into my pockets, hoping to find a weapon or something—anything!

My front pockets were empty, but I felt a tiny disc in my back pocket. It was one of Duncan's—the red one I had used in my fight with the giant spider! The one that made things *huge*.

Thank goodness I never washed my jeans.

I held the red disc tightly between my fingers and brought it up to my face. If I could stick it to me and turn it on, I'd blow up to the size of Godzilla and survive the fall.

But just before I could stick myself with it, Evil Ben and I crashed into the wall, sending us spiraling in circles.

I freaked out, grabbing the worm-eater with both of my hands.

The red disc stuck to his neck and activated.

Instantly, my evil twin expanded at superspeed, popping like a popcorn kernel. The force from his sudden growth shot me back up the shaft like a human cannonball.

I flew past the other worm-eaters, through the opening at the top, and out into the cold air of the night sky.

The academy looked tiny from so high up, but then it started getting bigger as my body hurtled toward it.

The alarm wailed as students gathered in the courtyard, most of them pointing at me.

I'd probably land in the trees somewhere on the other side of the school.

That was going to be messy.

Just then, a red blur shot from the courtyard to the top of the roof. It was Professor Duncan in his red hoodie using his forearm grappling hooks.

Everything happened in slow mo.

Duncan pointed his arm at me. A *POP!* cracked through the air. Suddenly a metal cable wrapped around my stomach and tightened. And then it yanked me down toward the roof right at the professor.

He ran to keep up with me, jumping to catch me right before impact. "I gotcha!"

Duncan didn't catch me, but he broke my fall . . . and his body.

I slammed into the roof with Professor Duncan's skeleton under me, shattering his bones, sending them flying.

Everything ached, but I was still alive. Duncan, on the other hand—

The professor's bones were scattered across the rooftop. I tried to put pieces back together, but they weren't connecting.

"Please! No, no, no!" I said desperately.

The mountain boomed and then fell silent. It happened again. And then again. My legs shook as I made my way to the edge of the roof.

Boom . . . silence.

Boom . . . silence.

Boom . . . silence.

In the distance, a dark shadow loomed over the trees. It rose and then fell again. It was the thing making the boom sounds. It was the thing shaking the mountain. It was the thing I had created when I stuck the red disc into its neck.

It was a ten-story monster.

And it was wearing my face.

CHAPTER FIFTY

From the roof, I saw frantic students running in the courtyard.

Abigail rode on Godzilla Ben's shoulder as he stormed the school grounds.

A group of kids ran toward him using their powers to attack the monster. Noah was with them, belching fireballs at the giant's foot.

Benzilla didn't even care. Do plants even feel pain?

"Noaaaaah!" I screamed, cupping my hands over my mouth, but he couldn't hear me.

Kepler was down there, too, but he was all the way across the courtyard, urging students to back away. Even if it was quiet, he was too far away to hear me.

I couldn't just stand on the roof while the rest of the school fought Benzilla. I had to help somehow.

I ran back to Duncan's shack, hoping to find something, anything, I could use to get the giant worm-eater's attention. The box of mystery discs sat next to the shack.

"*Pink disc, pink disc, pink disc,*" I murmured, rummaging through the box. The pink ones were bombs. Finally, I found one. "*Boo-yah-ha!*"

I set the disc down on the edge of the roof. Then I scooped up a handful of pebbles and chucked them at it.

One of the pebbles hit. The disc exploded with enough force to knock me off my feet. A burst of flaming red smoke bloomed as the roof blazed with fire.

"Whoops."

I looked at Abigail to see if it worked.

The fighting stopped for a moment as Abigail turned

toward the school, staring at the fire. The students in the courtyard also looked.

Benzilla changed direction and stomped toward me.

I waved my arms at Kepler, who was clear on the other side of the courtyard. He vanished into thin air and appeared by my side.

TELL ME, BEN, DO YOU HAVE A 100 FOOT TALL TWIN BROTHER YOU'VE KEPT SECRET FROM ME?

IT'S ONE OF ABIGAIL'S WORM-EATERS! IT'S, LIKE, SOME KIND OF PLANT OR SOMETHING! SHE'S BEEN KIDNAPPING KIDS ALL YEAR AND STORING THEM IN WEIRD EGG THINGIES, AND THEN SHE HOCKS A LOOGIE AND GROWS THEIR EVIL TWIN!

"That's *amazing*," he said.

"Yeah, not really the word *I'd* use to describe it," I said. "We found her secret lair *under your* secret lair, but she caught us, and, y'know, one thing led to another, and now we're facing off against Benzilla. Typical, right?"

"You were in my secret room?"

I smiled nervously. "Abigail knew about it, too."

Kepler looked back at Abigail. "Of course she did. She's always been the clever girl."

"She's crazy!"

The old man sighed, shaking his head slightly. "Sometimes the worst battles are in our own minds."

If I survived the night, I was gonna start a motivational-poster company and paste quotes from Kepler all over pictures of kittens.

Benzilla was almost to the Lodge. I hoped Kepler had a plan, because he seemed pretty calm about the whole thing.

"Noah and I found them all, but Abigail cornered us! She took Penny and then made a plant version of me!"

The old man squinted at the monster. "That thing must have taken *a lot* of saliva."

"Yeaaaaah, that part was my fault. I used one of Duncan's discs on it."

"The red one?"

I lowered my head like a guilty puppy. "The red one."

"Those *blasted* discs."

"Donald!" Abigail screamed from the shoulder of the monster. They were right next to the Lodge, close enough that I could see the whites of Abigail's crazy eyes. She was a big rubber band ball of psycho ready to snap at any second.

Kepler stood calmly on the very edge of the building,

the toes of his slippers hanging off the side. "Abigail Cutter . . ." he said. "What *have* you done?"

She panted heavily as she stared daggers at the headmaster of the school. "I found your secret!" she said. Benzilla said it at the exact same time, his voice booming. "You thought you could cover it up, but I *found* it! *I know everything!*"

Was she talking about the Kepler Cave?

"I know you did, my girl," Kepler said calmly, his voice old and exhausted. "I'm sorry you had to see any of that."

"Sorry doesn't change anything!" Abigail shrieked. "You destroyed me with your secret! You were supposed to help me, but all you did was hold me back! I *trusted* you! We *all* did!"

Kepler didn't raise his voice or show any anger. "I know. And I'm sorry."

"Everything we could've been . . . you've taken from us," Abigail said, tears streaming down her face. "And now I'm going to take it all back. I *won't* live in your shadow anymore!"

I was mesmerized. It was like I was watching the end of a movie I had missed the beginning of.

Or maybe it was the *beginning* of one. . . .

Kepler never took his eyes off Abigail. His face . . . he was sad. "You have no idea how much this has taken from me. . . ."

Abigail glared at the headmaster. "I could've been truly special."

Kepler nodded, reaching his hand out. "You *were* truly special. You were the most talented out of all of us."

"I've never hated anyone before. . . ." Abigail and the giant worm-eater said together, "But I hate *you.*"

Kepler lowered his hand.

"Do the others know?" Abigail asked, every word oozing with pain.

"No."

"They *will.* You were our hero. Now you're just a sad, selfish old man. I can't believe we allowed you to hold us back. Not anymore . . . *all* of the first fourteen will learn the truth."

The old man said nothing.

Abigail wiped tears from her face and straightened her posture. "Good-bye, Donald."

Benzilla's eyes narrowed. He lifted his truck-size fist and hammered down on the roof. Windows on the top floor burst, sending bits of glass raining down all over the courtyard.

Kepler disappeared and then reappeared instantly next to the fist. The monster balled his other hand and thundered down on another spot. Again, Kepler dodged it by moving at superspeed. It was so fast that it looked like he teleported.

The whole building shook as the giant played the deadliest game of Whac-A-Mole with the headmaster of the school.

I was a helpless wreck, unable to do anything because I'm just an eleven-year-old dork who wished he was a superhero.

Kepler dodged another shot, but the giant's other hand was already coming down. The old man got knocked back, violently tumbling across the roof.

Benzilla had punched the Lodge so hard that his gigantic hands were stuck between the ninth and tenth floors.

Donald Kepler lay perfectly still.

The giant pushed his arms deeper into the building, trying to pull it apart from the inside.

Part of the roof sunk, swallowing Duncan's shack. The fire spread to the top floors of the building.

The only place still intact was the spot under Kepler and me.

The monster freed one of his hands.

And that's when I saw it. The red disc stuck in the worm-eater's neck.

Kepler still wasn't moving.

Flames danced behind me.

Everyone watched in terror from the courtyard.

If Abigail won, she'd destroy the whole school and anybody left in it. She'd raise her army of supers and do something evil villainy, like take over the world.

And it was all my fault.

I made things worse by creating the monster. Kepler could've easily stopped Abigail if she didn't have a ten-story-tall worm-eater on her side.

It was just me on the roof. I was the only one who could stop her.

And then I had an idea. . . .

My three-point plan of attack was this:

JUMP ONTO BENZILLA'S ARM.

RIP OFF THE RED DISC.

3 ...

HERE LIES **BEN BRAVER,** BURIED IN THE TIGHTEST OF TIGHTYS AND THE WHITEST OF WHITEYS.

I wasn't a fan of number three, but . . . I didn't have a choice. Die at the hands of Benzilla or die saving everyone in the school.

I might never be a superhero, but I could still be a hero.

I thought about the last meal I ate with my parents—pizza. I was surprised I could remember my dad's words so well. . . .

"*. . . you have to promise me you'll be careful. Be smart. And most important . . . be safe. Don't do anything stupid. Stupid could get you hurt . . . or worse. Deal?*"

Eight months ago.

The last time I saw my parents.

I wished I could've seen them one last time.

The North Star shined brightly overhead. Somehow it made me feel more at peace.

Not *a lot*, but a *little*.

I wiped my eyes and stood my ground. "I'm sorry, Dad," I whispered, hoping that somehow he could hear me wherever he was. "But I'm about to do something stupid."

CHAPTER FIFTY-ONE

The heat of the fire crawled up my back. The building trembled as the roof fell apart behind me.

Students and teachers screamed at me from the courtyard. Well, not at *me* me, but the *giant* me crushing trees beneath his feet.

Still thinkin' about whether I was wearin' clean undies.

I was at the climax to my story. The showdown.

Either I win . . . or I die. Or I win *and* I die.

Dang it. Can't think about it.

I took several steps back. The edge of the roof was at least fifteen feet away. I was actually gonna do it. I was gonna jump off a ten-story building.

Can't think about it!

Thinking about it made my legs numb. What if I flubbed it up and just fell off the side?

Go already! Adam West would've gone already!

I sprinted for the monster. My foot hit the lip of the building and I leaped off the roof with everything I had.

It worked. I landed on Benzilla's arm. I grabbed at his shirt, but I barely caught hold, hanging from one hand.

Abigail saw me and laughed.

I climbed up the monster's arm. I couldn't look down. Looking down meant death.

My ten-story-tall evil twin pulled his other hand free from the Lodge. His body jerked backward away from the school.

He swatted at me with his good hand. I dodged it by swinging onto his back, where he couldn't reach.

The giant stumbled across the courtyard, trying to grab me with both hands. Students ran as Benzilla mashed the earth with his super huge feet.

I climbed higher until I was at the collar of his shirt.

"Ugh!" The horrid stench of worms and his slippery slug skin made me gag.

I pulled myself up and leaned into the giant's neck, making my way to the red disc.

I could see it. It was only a few feet away. All I had to do was reach out my hand and—

"Hey, Ben," Abigail said in an eerily jolly way. She was waiting for me, smiles and everything.

I lunged forward, reaching for the red disc, but Abigail kicked me square in the face. Pain surged through my body as everything started going black. I couldn't think. My nose hurt so bad I couldn't even open my eyes.

You just got kicked in the face by an adult. Things are not looking too good!

I slipped off the shirt collar, but I managed to grab it before plunging to my death. It made Abigail only try harder. She stood over me, stomping on my hand with her shoe.

"*Stop!*" I shouted.

Like *that* was gonna work.

Abigail ground her heel against the tendons in my hand. "None of this is actually happening to you! It's all just a bad dream, Ben! You're still in a coma at home! Just let go and wake up!"

I grabbed her ankle and tried to pull it off, but she was too strong. With one hand on the neck of the monster to keep her balance, she kept kicking at me.

And then I realized her hand *wasn't* on the neck of the monster, it was on the red disc. I couldn't rip the disc off myself, but maybe I could get Abigail to do it for me.

With Abigail's ankle still in my grip, I planted my feet and pulled *away* from the monster instead of trying to pull myself up.

She braced herself to keep from slipping off. As she did, her hand scraped the neck of the giant.

She stopped suddenly, confused. Her eyes went from me to her hand on Benzilla's neck. Little red flakes fell from her fingers as she opened them to see what she was holding.

She had crushed the disc.

But the monster was still ginormous! He wasn't shrinking like I thought he—oh, wait, nevermind.

Benzilla shrank just as fast as he had ballooned back in the cave, disappearing from beneath us. Abigail, the worm-eater, and I fell instantly.

"*Ben!*" I heard Noah yell. Weird that I could pick his voice out of a crowd of shouting students.

Ten stories down. That was how far I was falling. For someone who couldn't fly, I was spending a lot of time in the air.

Abigail flailed her arms and legs. The sound of terror coming from her mouth didn't sound human. It wasn't something I'll ever forget.

Evil Ben fell silently.

I wanted to scream, too, but I didn't.

I wasn't afraid.

I knew I was about to hit the ground, but at least I saved the school.

I actually saved lives.

I was the hero I always wanted to be.

I shut my eyes and hoped it wouldn't hurt.

The cold air burned my face, but then . . . it turned warm as I felt my body slow down in midair.

I opened my eyes to Noah's face beaming with a smile. He was holding me by my armpits.

We were flying! Well, *Noah* was flying. I was just catching a ride.

A stream of fire shot out likc rockets under his feet. His shoes were gone and the bottoms of his jeans were scorched. The stress of seeing me fall must have brought out more of his power.

"You can fly!" I said.

"And you owe me a new pair of shoes!" Noah joked.

But I didn't even care.

I'd buy Noah a million pairs of shoes for saving my life.

CHAPTER FIFTY-TWO

Noon.

Thursday.

It was the last day of school, exactly one month after the attack of the giant worm-eater.

Everyone sat on bleachers in the courtyard, watching the graduating class walk across a stage.

Headmaster Kepler sat in the front row. He was in pretty bad shape after Abigail's attack, but he seemed to be recovering just fine.

After Benzilla was defeated, Kepler fessed up and said he knew I'd stick around after Christmas because of my "unrelenting determination," but it was still a decision *I* had to make because *my path was mine to walk alone.* . . . I swear that man's like a walking fortune cookie.

He also told me that out of all the students to ever attend his school, I was the one who showed the most promise.

And I don't even have a power.

Nailed it.

Abigail survived, too. A bunch of trees broke her fall along with her bones. She was sent away to some kind of superprison or something. I wasn't supposed to know that, but Kepler told me anyway.

I told him Abigail said she was working with someone else, but that didn't surprise him, like he already knew or something. He believed Abigail was only one part of a larger machine.

Turns out Noah, Penny, and I dodged her worm-eater plan because we hung out on the roof most of the year messing with Duncan's gadgets.

Evil Ben met a terrible fate when his loogie-body splattered on the ground. The courtyard *still* reeked of worms because of that.

The students in the red eggs were awakened that night. Many of them had been asleep since the beginning of the school year, kept alive by the red egg yolks. Kepler gave them all passing grades, since, y'know . . . they were kidnapped by a villain.

Noah was now able to fly on command, the jerk.

Penny was fine. Upset that she missed all the action, but fine.

The Lodge was under construction. The monster-me had crushed the top two levels of the building. There was even talk of Kepler Academy needing to find a new home, but I think that had less to do with the construction and more to do with the fact that Abigail wasn't the only one who wanted a superpowered-kid army.

Kids had been trying to figure out what superpower I had finally discovered that helped me defeat Benzilla. My friends haven't told them that I actually *didn't* have a power. And Kepler assured me that he'd always keep that secret. He thought it was better that way.

Plus, I didn't mind the extra attention.

I had a fan club.

And Professor Duncan? Still alive and happier than ever. He became fully free from his physical body when I smashed into him. He went from being a skeleton to becoming a blue-and-white glow whose actual face we could see—like a real-life ghost.

Funny thing was that his ghost is the same age as he was when he "died," so he just looked like a kid.

I'm not sure what happened to his bones though. They're probably still on the roof.

Kepler was up at the mic, finishing his speech. I was too busy in my own head to notice that the ceremony was over.

The seniors threw their caps into the air. Several of them even shot their powers overhead to celebrate.

It was a decent end to a decent year.

CHAPTER FIFTY-THREE

School was officially out.

Self-driving Beetles had been picking up students all morning to take them home. Professor Duncan was helping them program destinations into the cars' GPSes. Even though he was a legit ghost, he was wearing clothes from back in his day.

My friends and I were out front, sitting with Brock.

All we needed to do was find an empty car, but we were stalling.

"Did Kepler ever say anything else about his secret room?" Jordan asked.

I shook my head. "He just ignored the question when I brought it up. Kept saying *'everything is as it should be, Benjamin.'* So whatever *that* means."

"He's hiding something. That room is like a treasure trove of unanswered questions," Penny said.

"Not really, if it's all fake photos and newspaper articles," I said.

"Then the question is, *why* he would do something like that," Penny said. "Plus, *something* about that room pushed Abigail's crazy button. Fake photos or not."

"But not *all* the photos were fake," Noah said. "It wouldn't make any sense for him to fake a fifteenth kid in the photo with the original fourteen. *That* photo was probably legit."

"So the *real* question is, what happened to *that* kid?" Jordan said. "Maybe *that's* what sent Abigail over the edge."

"What if *he's* the other villain she was working with?" Noah said.

We sat quietly for a moment, realizing there might've been more to that room than we first thought.

Penny broke the silence. She opened her backpack

and dug her hand around. "Oh, hey, Ben, I got you something. I sent some mice down to the city to get it for you."

She pulled out a crisp orange candy wrapper.

It was a peanut butter cup.

"It's not stolen," she added. "My mice left a buck on the counter."

I took the peanut butter cup and stared at it. I couldn't even remember the last time I had one.

"What's this for?" I asked.

"You know," Penny said, scraping the concrete with her foot. "For, like, savin' the school and, like, my life and stuff. Don't make a big deal about it."

Then she took a notebook out of her bag. "And I got this from the school bookstore. They didn't charge me cuz I told them it was for you."

It was a green sketchbook with Penny's handwriting on the cover. *Sketchbook of Secret Stuff 2*.

I choked up.

"Crybaby," Penny said with a smile. "You deserve it, though."

"I can't take *all* the credit," I said, setting the peanut butter cup on the stone snake. "Kepler's the one who really saved the day. You should've seen him on the roof! His superspeed was so sweet!"

"What's that?" Duncan said as he walked toward us. His voice sounded the way a violin would if a violin could talk. "What's this about Kepler's talent?"

"I was just saying how his superspeed is pretty cool," I said.

Duncan looked at me, puzzled. "Oh, no, his talent *isn't* superspeed."

"Uh, does he teleport then?" Jordan asked.

Duncan laughed and shook his head. "No, no, no, it's not teleportation, either. That man's power is *much* more specific. And *much* more extraordinary. He has the ability to literally—"

"Professor Duncan," Headmaster Kepler interrupted

as he suddenly appeared next to us. "I think I see some students in need of help with their cars."

Duncan looked over his shoulder. "Right. Sorry, Don."

"No need to be sorry," Kepler said, smiling.

Duncan jogged back to the line of VW Beetles.

"Does he even need to run like that?" Noah asked as he grabbed his bags. "Why doesn't he just float? Seriously! It's really confusing me right now!"

"We may never know," Kepler said. "Before Duncan's transition, I would've told you that abilities had to do with genetics and mutations, but how does a mutation keep his *energy* alive? He's *without* his body. *Without* DNA. It's fascinating."

Noah's eyes grew wide. "... *muy mago* ..."

Penny grunted. "Dude ... I know that means '*wizard*' in Spanish. ... Stop trying to be all slick."

Noah grinned.

The four of us said our good-byes and gave each other hugs and high fives. Penny took one last selfie of our whole group.

I was *not* looking forward to another fourteen-hour car ride.

Kepler helped me with my bags.

"Will I be allowed to return next year?" I asked. "I've got no powers, and half the school is destroyed because of me."

"Of course you can return next year. I chose you

because I saw something special in you. . . . I still wonder what it's going to be."

I looked at the old man with the scar. He believed my being at the school was for something *other* than saving it from Abigail?

I climbed into my small car, and Duncan helped me program the GPS and said good-bye. Kepler shut the door, and the VW Beetle immediately started.

My ride pulled forward and sped down the road. I watched out the back window until the school disappeared around the curve of the mountain.

I didn't want to leave.

Summer vacation was three months. I'd have to wait three *long* months until my second year at the academy . . . until my sequel.

I wasn't even a minute away from Kepler Academy, but I already missed my friends. I couldn't wait to go back.

I unzipped my bag and dug my hand in. At least I finally got my peanut butter cups that Penny—oh no . . .

I pressed my face against the cold window.

My peanut butter cups were still on the stone snake.

. . . Flippin' eggs.

ACKNOWLEDGMENTS

Connie Hsu, my super talented editor, for helping me sound like I know what I'm doing. Simon Boughton, for supporting and standing behind the book. Megan Abbate, for going above and beyond. Elizabeth Clark, for making everything look so good.

Dan Lazar, my agent, for absolutely everything. Torie Doherty-Munro, Cecilia de la Campa, and all the other amazing people at Writers House who seem to work all hours of the night.

Camye, my wife, for putting up with all my childish and immature jokes, for pushing me to chase after dreams, and for being my best friend. My kids, Evie, Elijah, Parker, and Finn, for making me take video game breaks and for keeping me on my toes so I can stay young forever.

And my parents, for letting me stay up late to watch all the best movies, which also reminds me to thank Marty McFly, Mikey Walsh, Jack Burton, David Freeman, Alex Rogan, Bill S. Preston Esq., and Ted "Theodore" Logan.

GOFISH

MARCUS EMERSON

What did you want to be when you grew up?
An astronaut. Sadly, that never panned out. Maybe someday, though.

When did you realize you wanted to be a writer?
In eighth grade. After I saw *Jurassic Park*, I wrote the sequel in one of my notebooks. It was about six pages long. Spielberg never ended up using my draft, but to be fair I never sent it to him. Maybe I was too afraid of success that early in life. I mean, if I make it to the top of the mountain in eighth grade, where do I go from there?

What was your favorite thing about school?
The field trips because they were adventures with my friends outside of a school setting.

What were your hobbies as a kid? What are your hobbies now?
My hobby as a kid was art, and I'm very proud to say that not only is it still my hobby, it's also my job.

What was your first job, and what was your "worst" job?
McDonald's was my first job at sixteen. I was the guy in the back, accidentally messing up everybody's orders because of how busy it always was. "Oh, you wanted MEAT on your cheeseburger? My bad." And my worst job—I once worked a single day on a hog farm in the middle of summer. That was a rough day . . .

What book is on your nightstand now?
It's a mix of *Calvin and Hobbes*, *FoxTrot*, and *Garfield*.

How did you celebrate publishing your first book?
I don't remember exactly, but it's very likely that we went out for ice cream the day it was published . . . and then everyday afterward for a week, maybe two.

Where do you write your books?
On the beat-up, old couch in my office. It's cozy and sits right in front of the TV so I can watch cartoons with my kids during my breaks.

What sparked your imagination for *The Super Life of Ben Braver*?
X-Men was one of the first comics I owned so it'll always have a special place in my heart, especially the stories when a new mutant joins the school. So, with Ben Braver, I thought— what would it look like if a random kid without powers went there, too?

What is your favorite word?
Indubitably. It's just so fun to say!

If you could live in any fictional world, what would it be?
Uh, the *Star Wars* galaxy! Do I even need to explain why??

What was your favorite book when you were a kid? Do you have a favorite book now?
As a kid, any of the Goosebumps books—they're the first books I couldn't put down. I'd start and finish one in the same day. As an adult, it's always changing, and there are many different reasons that come into play besides it being "a good book." Right now, it's *The Lord of the Rings*—it's a GREAT book, but I suspect it's my current favorite because I'm reading it out loud to my daughter at bedtime.

If you could travel in time, where would you go and what would you do?
I'd travel back to when dinosaurs existed—the monstrously HUGE ones. And then I'd find a safe place to hide and just watch them do their dinosaur things.

What's the best advice you have ever received about writing?
That I need to FINISH the book for it to get better. Once it's finished, it's easier to see what parts work or, more importantly, what parts DON'T work, and that's critical when going back and fixing scenes.

What advice do you wish someone had given you when you were younger?
Start sooner. Starting is the hardest part. Whatever you want to do, you'll wish you had started sooner. Ever since I was in second grade, I knew I wanted to be a professional artist, but I didn't start until I was 30.

Do you ever get writer's block? What do you do to get back on track?

I rarely get writer's block because I meticulously map out every detail of a scene before I write. When I DO get stuck, I go back to the drawing board and re-map the scene I'm having trouble with.

What do you want readers to remember about your books?

I'm happy if my books can make readers laugh out loud. I don't take myself too seriously, and neither do my characters—a little bit of joy is all I want to spread.

If you were a superhero, what would your superpower be?

I'd stop time. There was this show I used to watch as a kid where a girl could stop time by putting her fingers together. I could pull the most epic pranks if I had that power.

Does Ben Braver actually have a superpower?

Are there more evil villains
lurking in their midst?

And will he ever eat his peanut butter cup?

Keep reading for an excerpt.

PROLOGUE

Sixty miles per hour.

The top speed of a Vespa scooter.

I'm not a doctor, but I don't think sixty miles an hour is fast enough to outrun an exploding atom bomb.

Headmaster Kepler was riding passenger, shouting instructions on how to "operate a vehicle," his words.

"I know how to drive a scooter!" I shouted, cranking the Vespa's handle so hard that it snapped. "Oh, farts . . ."

So there we were, coasting on a dying scooter, seconds away from an atomic explosion that would take out Kepler Academy and the city of Lost Nation.

I can confidently say that was the worst day of my short, little life.

Thousands were about to die.

All my friends were about to die.

I was about to die.

And it was 100 percent my fault. . . .

CHAPTER ONE

I sat alone in the passenger seat of a self-driving Volkswagen Beetle.

Summer was over, and I was headed back to Kepler Academy—a super secret school for kids with superpowers.

It was like the X-Mansion, but without all the spandex.

A whole summer had passed since I saved the academy from an army of plant people created by a woman named Abigail Cutter.

She was all kinds of crazy.

With a loogie, some dirt, and a strand of your hair, Abigail could grow your evil twin, which she controlled with her mind.

They were horrifying plant zombies who ate earthworms by the handful, or as the greatest scientific minds called them, worm-eaters.

ARISE, MY BABIES!

Premium-grade nightmare fuel.

My car had been driving all day, so the school had to be close. It should've been all Colorado mountains and trees outside my window.

But it wasn't.

An empty desert wasteland stretched out for miles on all sides of me.

"Computer, where am I?" I asked.

The GPS didn't answer because I don't live in a *Star Trek* movie.

The clock showed 1 a.m.

"Flippin' eggs, are you serious?" I muttered.

I should've been at Kepler Academy hours ago! What was my car thinking driving through the desert at *one in the stupid idiot morning*?

The VW sputtered to a stop. The headlights died slowly, leaving me alone in the dark. My door unlocked and popped open by itself.

I looked for the North Star, but it was cloudy. My dad and I have this thing—whenever I'm scared, all I have to do is find that star. We both look at it every night; it's like our way of saying "I miss you" to each other even if we're in different places.

Doesn't work when it's cloudy, though.

I stared at the empty desert outside my car.

And that's when I heard it—the sloppy, chomping sounds of worm-eaters.

I grabbed the edge of the car door to shut it, but instead of metal . . . I felt somebody's fingers.

Worm-eaters burst from the darkness, sprinting toward me. No screams. No grunts. Just moist feet slapping the dry desert crust.

The hand at my door grabbed my wrist and yanked me into the air until I was face-to-face with her.

It was Abigail Cutter.

Mangled worms fell from her nasty, chapped lips as her fingers morphed into thick vines that slithered around my neck, suffocating me.

I shot forward, eyes shut, drenched in cold sweat, screaming at the top of my lungs. I tried to push Abigail away, but when I opened my eyes . . .

She was gone.

I was still in my bed at home.

I'll say it again: nightmare fuel.

. . . what the jibs was wrong with me?

I pushed the blankets aside and looked out my window. Still black, but that's how it is when you need to get on the road by 4 a.m.

Mom flipped on the light. "Oh, good, you're up! Your car's outside!" she said, excited for my second year at Kepler Academy. Way more excited than I was.

When I left the academy last year, I was the baddest hero ever, but all that disappeared once I got home.

Every time I closed my eyes at night, I saw wormeaters. I spent most nights wide awake, staring at my door until the sun came up.

My parents didn't know about the nightmares.

Or much of anything that happened last year.

Including the fact that I was powerless—the *only* powerless kid at Kepler Academy.

They asked me all summer to spill the beans, but all I ever said was, *"It was fun,"* because saying, *"I jumped off a ten-story building to save the school from a Godzilla-size plant zombie,"* would've given them a panic attack.

Or maybe it would've given *me* one.

I had spent the last three months dodging their questions by mowing lawns morning till night, every single day.

The work helped keep my mind off worm-eaters, and I liked the extra cash, too. I thought about blowing it all on a mountain of peanut butter cups, but instead I saved up and bought myself something nice.

After getting dressed and scraping a toothbrush across my teeth, I went outside.

Mom stood by the Kepler car as Dad tossed my bags into the trunk.

"That'll do it," Dad said, messing my hair up. "Don't come home this time without a power!"

I knew he was joking—that he only said it because he believed I already had come back with a power.

. . . joke's on him though, right?

Ugh.

Mom knelt and gave me a hug, but I just stood there like a stiff doll.

She pulled back. "Are you all right?"

"I guess," I said, but she saw through me.

"Hey, it'll be okay. You've already done this once. Going back will be like riding a bike. Once you're there, you'll hardly miss home at all."

"Even though we'll be missing *you* like crazy," Dad added.

I didn't want them to know I was scared, but I wasn't good at hiding it.

Mom hugged me tighter. "I know this is hard for you, but you need to know that it's harder for me. I don't want you to go, Ben. I want you to stay here and go to a boring school and sit around our boring house at night, but we both know you can't."

Dad put his hand on my head while I squeezed my mom.

"But . . . I'm scared," I said honestly.

Mom smiled. "Nothing wrong with that. I'm scared, too. Scared that something terrible will happen to you while you're gone."

Like jumping off a ten-story building.

"Being scared just means you get to be brave," Mom said. "Because we both know you have to go back. You belong there. People spend their entire lives looking for a greater destiny, but yours knocked at our door and invited you to come out to play. We might not know exactly why yet, but you *belong* at *that* school."

She was right.

I had to go back.

For her.

For my dad.

For all the students at the academy.

I was the hero who saved the school last year.

And what kind of hero goes into hiding after something like that?